KB154701

아, 아
Ah, Ah

아, 아
Ah, Ah

박소원 한영시집

Park So Won's Korean-English Poetry Collection

여국현 옮김

Translated by Yeo Kook Hyun

곰곰나루

시인의 말

드디어 한영시집을 펴낸다. 삼십대 후반쯤이었다. 제임스 조이스의 『율리시스』 출간을 후원했던 실비아 비치, 그의 서점 '셰익스피어 앤 컴퍼니'에 관한 이야기를 읽었다. 그 무렵에 글을 쓰는 꿈을 가졌다.

최승자의 시 "내가 더 이상 나를 죽일 수 없을 때 / 내가 더 이상 나를 죽일 수 없는 곳에서 / 혹, 내가 피어나리라"(「이제 가야만 한다」에서)는, 문학이 어쩌면 나를 구원할지도 모른다는 희망을 갖게 했다. 고통스러운 찰나마다 꿈과 희망이 꿈틀거렸다. 홀로 자주 슬펐다.

그 사이 시인이 되었다. 3권의 창작시집과 한중시집 『修飾哭聲:울음을 손질하다』, 한러시집 『예니세이 강가에서 부르는 이름』을 출간했다. 그리고 이 한영시집 『아,아』에 이르기까지 내 안의 '상처'를 너무 많이 건드려왔다. 상처와 상처 사이에서 본 얼굴들이 점점 선명해졌다.

종종 무슨 재미로 사냐고 묻는 사람들이 있다. 꽃이 피고 달이 뜨듯, 나는 '당신'을 읽고 '당신'을 쓴다. 상처의 다른 표정은 그리움이

었을까. 그 위에 비가 내리고 눈이 내리는 동안 '당신'을 바라보는 낙으로 살았다.

읽고 쓰는 시간이 차곡차곡 축적되는 하루다. 틈틈이 훅 훅 침입하는 외로움 고독이여, 내내 내게 머물러주시길!

2024년 7월
동탄 반송동 나루마을에서
박소원

Poet's Words

Finally, I am publishing a Korean-English poetry collection of mine. It was in my late thirties, when I read a story about Sylvia Beach, who sponsored the publication of James Joyce's *Ulysses*, and her and her bookstore, 〈Shakespeare & Company〉. Around that time, I dreamt of writing.

Some phrases of Choi Seung Ja's poem, "When I can no longer kill myself / Where I can no longer kill myself / Perhaps, I shall bloom" (from "I Must Go Now") gave me hope that perhaps literature could save me. In every painful moment, dreams and hopes stirred. I was often sad alone.

In the meantime, I became a poet. I published three volumes of original poetry, a Korean-Chinese poetry collection, *修飾哭聲: Trimming the Cry* and a Korean-Russian poetry collection *Names Sung by the Yenisei River*. And until the Korean-English poetry collection *Ah, Ah*(2024), I've touched upon too many 'wounds' within myself. The faces I saw between the wounds became increasingly clearer.

Sometimes people often ask me what kind of fun I live for. Just as flowers bloom and the moon rises, I read 'you' and write 'you.' Could another expression of wounds have been longing? I lived in the joy of looking at 'you' while rain and snow fell on it.

My days consist of accumulating reading and writing time one by one. Oh, loneliness and solitude that sneak in every now and then! Please stay with me forever.

July 2024

from Naru Village, Bansong-dong, Dongtan

Park So Won

차례

Table of Contents

2부

Part II

3부

Part III

4부

Part Ⅳ

1부
Part Ⅰ

이 세상을 사랑하는 법

큰 강줄기를 따라 한 달 가량 모닥불을 피우고 취사를 하며 북을 두드려 커다란 코끼리를 몰아간다 유일한 묘수는 휘파람 소리로 포식자를 부르는 것, 양철 지붕 위로 도토리 떨어지는 소리 같은 갈대숲을 휘도는 바람 같은 소리를 부드럽게 낼 것 도토리가 우는 것일까 갈대가 웃는 것일까 제 귀를 의심할 때까지 유유히 소리를 흘려보낼 것 달도 뜨지 않는 날, 누구의 손도 잡을 수 없는 거리까지 제 몸에서 새어나오는 소리처럼 느껴질 때까지 나무가 빽빽하게 들어선 정글로 들어설 때까지 휘파람을 분다 머리를 쓰는 것은 금물, 손대지 말고 그. 렇. 게. 갈 때까지 가야 마지막이 치명적인 한판을 노릴 수 있다 그리고 조금씩 조금씩 밀림으로 털끝 같은 소리 내지 말고 밤낮으로 불을 지피며 북을 두드리며 느릿느릿 강물처럼 자연스러운 휘파람 소리를 흘려보내야 한다

결국, 그가 말 울음소리를 낼 때까지
어린나무를 송두리째 뽑아버릴 때까지

How to Love This World

For about a month, following the currents of a great river, lighting a bonfire, cooking, and beating a drum, I am driving a large elephant. The only trick is to call out predators with a whistle and to softly make a sound like the wind blowing through a reed forest, similar to the sound of acorns falling on a tin roof. Is the acorn crying or the reed laughing? Let the sound flow gently until I doubt my ears. On the night when the moon doesn't rise, I whistle until I enter a jungle full of trees, to the distance where no one's hand can be reached, and feel that the sound is leaking from my body. It is forbidden to use my head. Without touch, go to the utmost as far as you can, and you can expect and aim for the final, fatal match. And little by little, into the jungle, without making any sound, but by lighting fires and beating drums day and night, slowly, let the natural whistle flow off like a river;

In the end, until he makes the sound of a horse's cry,
Until he pulls out all the young trees.

아, 아

내 입에서는 언제부터인가
세 사람의 목소리가
튀어나온다

뇌졸중으로 돌아가신 어머니와 태어나서 삼 개월을 살았다는 언니와
마흔에 목매달아 죽은 내 친구, 내 목소리 속 또 다른 목소리들 섞여 나온다

새 발자국 위에
토끼 발자국
토끼 발자국 위에
노루 발자국
노루 발자국 위에
코끼리 발자국처럼
작은 목소리 위에
큰 목소리들이
먼지처럼 덧쌓여간다

비 내리는 창가에 앉아 휘파람을 불거나
주방에서 오리 훈제구이를 굽고 있거나

나에게는 당신의 질병이 유전되고 있다

목소리들, 저승을 이승처럼 이승을 저승처럼 쉴 새 없이 비벼댄다 두고 간 남은 생이 얼마나 그리웠으면 여행지의 마지막 밤까지 따라붙는 거니? 룸메이트는 밤중에 고양이 울음소리가 기분 나쁘다며 창문을 건다 걸쇠를 채운다

이국의 밤은 생수로
칼칼한 목구멍을 헹구고
창밖은 건기의 계절이
슬쩍 우기로 바뀌었다
아, 아
참혹한 전쟁에 패한 병사처럼
거칠고 지친 목소리 아, 아

Ah, Ah

From my mouth, for some time now,
voices of three people
spring forth.

My mother, who passed away from a stroke, my sister, who lived for only three months after birth,
and my friend who hung himself at forty, their voices mix with mine and emerge from within.

Like elephant footprints
on top of deer footprints
on top of rabbit footprints
on fresh snow,
large voices
pile up on the small ones
like layers of dust.

I, Sitting by the window on a rainy day whistling,
or cooking duck confit in the kitchen,
your diseases are being passed down to me.

Voices, tirelessly blending the hereafter with the here and now, the here and now with the hereafter, how much must they have missed the life they left behind to cling to me until the last night of a journey? My roommate closes the window in the middle of the night, finding the sound of a cat's cry unsettling, and locks it.

The night in a foreign land washes my spicy throat with bottled water,

and outside, the dry season
slyly turns into the rainy season.
Ah, ah,
like a soldier defeated in a terrible war,
a rough and tired voice, ah, ah.

봄에게 무슨 일이 생겼는가

햇살 눈부신 대낮에도 부음이 온다 새는 휘파람 같은 울음으로 날아갔다 칼날을 기억하는 손목이 주머니 속에서 아프다 그렇게 아름다운 말은 나에게 씨부렁거리지 마

그 무렵 한참 좋을 나이에 우리는 추위 속에서 어둠으로 갈라졌다 끊임없이 새 울음소리로 진동하는 시간, 나는 한쪽 가슴만 내어주고 살기로 했다 바닥에 바짝 엎드려 있을 때에도 가슴은 오른쪽보다 왼쪽이 문득 높다

헌 자동차는 중고매매 시장에서 줄 서서 낡아간다 친구의 오토바이를 빌려 타고 온 소년이 커다란 가방을 내려놓는다 면도날로 밀어낸 종아리의 털처럼 쓸데없는 기억들은 대낮에도 검게 자라난다

그러나 기억은 짝가슴 속에서도 균형을 잃어간다 도시에서 도시로 건너가는 버스 안에서 문득 눈물이 터졌다 왼쪽 가슴으로만 스며들던 새들의 휘파람소리가 차 안에 가득하다 승객들은 조금씩 졸기 시작한다

한쪽 눈만 뜨고 다리 위를 지나간다 강 위를 선회하는 새들, 꽁무니를 쫓아간다 자주 한을 날리는 눈빛들, 짙푸른 물 위에서 솜사탕처럼 달게 녹아간다

What Did Happen to Spring?

Even in the bright sunlight of daytime, an obituary arrives. The Bird flew away with a cry like a whistle My wrist remembering the blade aches in my pocket. Don't say such a beautiful word to me.

During those high times, we split into darkness in the cold. In a time vibrating incessantly with the birds' crying, I decided to live giving half of my heart. Even when I'm lying flat on the ground, my left chest is suddenly higher than my right one.

Used cars are getting old, lining up in the second-hand market. A boy who comes on a borrowed motorcycle from his friend's puts down a large bag. Unnecessary memories, like leg hairs shaved with a razor blade, grow black even in broad daylight.

But memories lose their balance even within an uneven chest. Tears burst out suddenly on a bus moving from city to city. The sound of birds' whistles, permeating only into my left chest, fills the bus. Passengers start to doze off little by little.

I am crossing a bridge with one eye open, following the birds circling above the river. Eyes often reflecting 'Han'*, melting sweetly like cotton candy on the blue-black water.

* 'Han' is a word that means deep sadness or regret in Korean.

능소화야 능소화야

바람은 높은 곳에서부터
거래를 트기 시작했다

군데군데 죽은 핏물들
지붕까지 오른 줄기들 뜯겨지고 있다

허공의 발자국들 담장 틈마다
발을 들여놓고 주춧돌까지 내려간다

나는 거추장스러운 비밀처럼
불안한 꿈처럼 뜯겨지고 있다

짓뭉개진 꽃잎들
한 묶음씩 마당에 뿌려진다

바람의 지뢰, 어둠의 지뢰 위에
다시 실패하라 더 실패하라*

내 몸이 짐이다, 팔순 넘으신 노모처럼
얼결에 휘갈겨 쓴 합의서가 몇 백 장인가

민박집 마당에서 자꾸 능숙해지는 질 나쁜 거래
언제나 나를 버리게 하는 것은 나였다

밤이 새도록 빠른 리듬에 맞추어 추는
경쾌한 죽음의 댄스 댄스

나는 너를 모른다 나는 너를 모른다
수시로 나는 너를 부정한다

문득 밤이 경쾌한 리듬에 맞추어
마당 밖으로 신사처럼 물러나고 있다

안녕하세요? 안녕하세요?
새들은 백리 밖에서도 노래를 부르고 있나 보다

이보다 혹독한 밤이면 어떤가
보라!

태풍 속 바람들 떨어진 꽃잎마다
제각각 날개를 달아주고 있지 않는가

*Samuel Beckett의 *Nohow On*(1989) : 진은영 시 「나에게」에서

Oh, Trumpet Creeper, Trumpet Creeper!

From high places, the wind
begins to open trade.

Here and there, dead bloodstains,
the vines climbing to the roofs are tearing apart.

Footprints in the air, every gap in the fence
step in and go down to the cornerstone.

I am being ripped off
like an cumbersome secret, like an anxious dream.

Crushed petals
are scattered in bunches across the yard

On the landmines of the wind, the mines of darkness,
fail again, fail more.

My body is a burden, like my mother over eighty.
How many hundreds of pages are the unwittingly scribbled agreements!

〉

In the guesthouse yard, the bad trades getting more skilled;
It was always me who abandoned myself.

The tripping dance of death, dance
dancing to a fast rhythm all night.

I don't know you, I don't know you;
I frequently deny you.

Suddenly, to the jaunty rhythm
the night is retreating out of the yard like a gentleman.

Hello? Hello?
Perhaps the birds are singing from a hundred miles away.

What if the night were harsher than this?
Look!

Is the wind within the typhoon giving each fallen petal
its own wings?

* 'Quoted in the poem "To Me" by Jin Eun Young, from Samuel Beckett's *Nohow On*

지렁이

몸을 대보면 길마다 온도가 다르다
길은 제 체온으로 구불구불 혹은 직선으로
나를 부르고 있었구나
무심코 한 응답들이 내 길이구나
장마가 이렇게 쉽게 끝날 줄도 모르고
음습한 흙 속의 길을 서둘러 떠나왔으므로
내가 떠나온 길이 멀리서 더 멀리
멀어져가는 것을
화단의 자귀나무 너머로 뒤돌아볼 뿐,
애초의 제 온도를 잃고
쉽게 몸을 바꾸는 땅 속의 길을
오금이 저리도록 감지하고 있을 뿐,
아무리 뒤돌아보아도
한번 떠나온 길은
내가 결코 갈 수 없는 길이다
비가 그치고 달궈지기 시작하는 아파트 주차장에서
방향을 잃고 벌겋게 익고 있는 몸
내 몸이 내 길이다
제 체온을 잃은 징글징글한 몸을
자동차 바퀴에 신음도 없이
터져버린 나의 몸, 반 토막을

햇살이여, 지금도 눈여겨보는가

Earthworm

As I touch it, every road has a different temperature.
The road has been leading me windingly or straightly
Depending upon its temperature,
Mindless responses are my path.
Not expecting the rainy season to end so easily,
As I hurriedly left the damp way under the earth,
I only look back at the road I left
Grows ever distant,
Seen from afar,
Over the garden's silk trees;
And feeling only the underground path,
Easily losing its original temperature,
Tingling in my legs,
No matter how much I look back,
The road I've ever left
Is one I can never return to.
In the scorching parking lot after the rain stopped,
My body, losing direction, being reddened and heating up,
Is my path.
In the scorching parking lot after the rain stopped,
My body, losing its temperature and feeling distressed,

Exploded in half under the car's wheels

Without a groan, my half-body,

O Sun, are you still watching?

매미

나뭇가지와 가지의 틈새와 끼어
마음과 마음을 미닫이창처럼 여닫고 앉아서
한 시절을 통째로 보내었다
매 앰 매 앰 매 애 앰
발음막이 터지도록 무시로
낯선 소리가 줄줄 새는 몸의 균열을
들여다보면서
오늘도 울음으로 살아내는 법을
한 마디씩 배우고 있다
삶의 본능처럼 작동되는
울음의 센서가 몸과 연결되어 움직이는 것을
혼자서 조용히 감지할 뿐,
낮에는 나무껍질 밑에 숨어 있다가
밤이 되면 튀어나오는 수상한 울음소리들
실은 나를 다 털어서 걸고 하는
절박한 게임이라는 것을 눈치 채는 이는 아무도 없다
자신을 다 걸고 덤벼들어도
고작 하루를 살아내는 일이어서야
쯧쯧쯧, 도박 치고는 스스로에게 조금은 미안하다
내 배는 빈 동굴처럼 생겼지
모든 운동의 중심을 아랫배에만 두고

움직이고 있는 이 소란스런 시간들
저 푸른 화투 패 사이를 비집고
결국, 이 여름 내내 펼쳐지는 올인하는 울음소리

Cicada

Tucked between branches and gaps,
Opening and closing hearts like sliding doors,
I spend an entire season.
Mae-em Mae-em Me-e-em,*
At any time, until my vocal cords burst from strain,
Looking into the cracks in my body
Where strange sounds escape,
Today, too, word by word
I'm learning the art of living through crying.
The strange sounds of crying,
Quietly detecting the sensor of crying
Which operates like the instinct of life
To move linking with the movement of the body,
And hiding under the bark of the trees during the day,
And pops out at night,
No one realizes this is a desperate game
Played by risking all of me.
Even throwing itself all in,
It is just to live out a day,
Tut tut tut, I feel a bit sorry for myself for a gamble.
My belly looks like an empty cave.

These noisy times moving,

When focusing the center of all movements

On the lower abdomen;

Wedging through the blue cards of hwatoo**

Finally, the all-in cries unfolding throughout this summer.

*Onomatopoeia that expresses the sound of cicadas crying in Korean like 'chirp' in English.

**An East Asian card game played with 48 cards that represent months or seasons.

푸른 뿌리

— 양파

뿌리 뽑히는 순간 이미 중심을 잃었다
베란다 한 귀퉁이에 걸려서도
중심 없는 나는 잘 지낸다
겨울 햇볕에 뿌리를 건조시키며
나는 정말 잘 지낸다 잘 썩고 있다
몸속으로 꺾어 들어오는 햇빛들
내 장기 곳곳을 누비고 돌아다닌다
희망은 늘 오전에서 오후로 넘어간다
주기가 바뀌는 각각의 달빛을
한 스푼씩 더 먹으며
겹겹이 투명한 몸을, 베란다 회색 벽에
문지르며 깎으며 나는 본다,
갈수록 자꾸만 진물이 흐르는 목숨을,
갈수록 징그러운 벌레들이 몰려드는 내일을,
썩은 몸이 텅텅 비어 먼지가 일 때까지
매운 성깔을 망 밖으로 몰아내며
나는 본다, 진물 나는 몸 밖으로 돋는

푸른 싹들을 나는 본다
남은 내 목숨들 모두 내놓으면
너, 내 새로운 뿌리가 되어줄래*

내가 몸 밖 나에게 가만가만 물어본다
나처럼 썩어 뭉개지는 미래가
자꾸만 보이지만……,

*김충규의 시 「내 고양이는 지금 어느 골목에 있을까」의 패러디

Blue Roots

— Onion

The moment I was uprooted, I had already lost my center.
Hanging on a edge of the balcony,
I am doing well without a center.
Drying my roots in the winter sunlight,
I'm really doing well, rotting away well.
The sunbeams that bend into my body,
Wander and stride through my organs.
Hope always moves from morning to afternoon.
Eating a spoonful more of moonlight as the moon changes its cycle,
Rubbing and peeling the transparent layers of my body
On the veranda's gray wall, I see.
The more time passes, the more my life oozes pus,
The more creepy bugs gather towards tomorrow,
Until my rotten body is hollowed out and dust rises,
I drive out my spicy temper beyond the net,
I see. The blue sprouts
Sprouting out of my pus-oozing body
I see them.
If I were to give you all my remaining life,
Will you become my new root?*

I quietly ask myself outside my body.
Though a future, rotting and squashing like me,
Keeps becoming visible……,

*A parody of Kim Chung gyu's poem "Where Might My Cat Be Now, in Which Alley?"

나는 다시

손가락 지문마다 거센 돌개바람이 돈다
나는 다시 한 자리에서 움직이지 않고
지나간 사랑에 대해서 침묵한다
궁금한 방향으로 호기심을 튕기며
길이 뻗어가듯
새들은 서쪽 허공으로 날아간다
나는 다시 뿌리에 힘을 주고
태풍이 한반도를 빠져나가는 동안
사람들은 내 말을 믿지 않고 내가 내 말을 안 믿는다*
뿌리 뽑힌 주목나무 곁에서
나는 다시 벌벌 떨었다
자꾸만 무서운 그의 과거가 보인다
캄캄한 저녁이 내 안의 엘리베이터를 타고
다시 지상으로 내려오는 동안
과거에게 듣고 싶은 말이 참 많았다
나이테를 휘도는 불안을 토악질하며
계절이 다시 지나간다
홀쭉해진 허공의 옆구리에 가지를 걸치고
나는 다시 나이를 먹는다
적당하게 친한 사람에게 배신을 당하고
새들은 서녘의 말을 물고

떠난 자리로 다시 돌아온다
마른 가지마다 먼 곳의 말들이 새잎을 틔운다
흔들리는 삼월의 그림자가 푸릇푸릇하다.

*김수영의 시 「거짓말의 여운 속에서」에서

I, Once Again

Fierce whirlwinds swirl around each fingerprint.
I remain motionless in one spot, again,
And silent about past love.
Flicking curiosity towards intriguing directions,
Birds fly into the western sky.
As the path stretches out ahead of me,
I give strength to my roots again,
While the typhoon is passing through the Korean peninsula,
People don't believe my words, and I don't believe mine.*
Beside an uprooted yew tree
I trembled again.
His terrifying past keeps haunting.
While the dark evening takes the elevator inside me
Coming back down to the ground,
I have so many things I want to hear from the past.
Vomiting the anxiety that swirls around the tree rings,
The season passes again.
Leaning a branch against the thinned side of the void,
I'm getting old again.
Betrayed by someone moderately close,
Birds carry the words of the west,

Coming back to where they left.

On each dry branch, words from afar sprout new leaves,

The shadows of the swaying March are green and vivid.

*from "In the Afterglow of Lies" by Kim Soo Young

움

한 곳에 너무 오래 앉아 있었을까
몸에 밴 습기를 날려 보내지도 못하고
나는 내 나이의 무게보다 더 무겁다
무성한 잎을 매달고 가지를 치켜들고
오래 서 있었던 옛 기억으로
수시로 다리에 힘이 들어간다
변함없이 한 자리를 지키며 서 있기란
여간 어려운 일이 아니어서
수직의 기억으로 온종일 신음이 내려간다
얼었다 녹았다를 반복하며
나보다 먼저
내 신음소리를 듣게 되는
체온의 균형을 잃어가는 이는 누구인가
온도의 균형을 잃어버린 이들은
온기 중에 가장 따뜻한 온기가
사람의 온기라고 몸 붙이고 앉는다
사람들은 변함없는 품성처럼
언제나 한 방향을 고집한다
눈송이들 한나절 앉았던 자리가
밤이 되면 시간처럼 더욱 깊어진다

Sprout

Have I been sitting in one place for too long?
Unable to blow away the moisture settled in my body.
I am heavier than the weight of my age,
Weighted down by lush leaves, supporting branches
Due to the old memories of standing still for so long
My legs are periodically stiff.
As standing in one place without change
Is not an easy task,
Groan descends upon as vertical memories all day.
Repeating between freeze and thaw;
Who is the one
To hear my groans before me,
And lose the balance of temperature?
Those who have lost their balance of temperature
Sit close together,
Knowing that the warmest warmth is human warmth;
People, in their unchanging nature,
Always insist on one direction. strive in
The place where the snowflakes sat for half a day,
Deepens like the time, when night comes.

무제

지하에서 나온 상품이 바다를 건너간다

인형의 눈 위에 동전을 올려주는 손

캄캄한 꿈을 꾸었다

땅만 보고 걸어가는 꿈

손에서 손으로 옮겨지는 꿈

일톤 트럭에 실려 가는 꿈

꿈은 깨면 그만인데 앞이 캄캄한 게 마음이 상했다

동전으로 눈을 가린 인형처럼

보이는 게 모두 검은 색이었다

Untitled

Products from underground cross the sea

A hand placing a coin over the eyes of a doll

I had a dark dream;

A dream of walking with eyes fixed on the ground

A dream that passed from hand to hand

A dream transported in a one-ton truck

The dream ended when I woke up, but I still felt hurt by the darkness

It's all right to wake up from my dreams, but I was hurt by there was no hope

Like a doll with its eyes covered by coins

Everything I saw was black

썩는 것에 대하여

1

사과, 책상 위에서 썩었다
물큰한 단내 속에서 구더기들 바글거렸다
어느새 구더기가 빨갛게 배를 내밀고
통통한 배로 달큰한 물을 밀며 나아가는
저 집요한 움직임
다음날 방문을 열어보니 어느 결에
날개를 편다 난다
책에, 책상에, 피아노에 앉아
벌써 휴식을 취하고 여유를 즐기는가
사과는 물컹한 제 몸을 구더기로 채워가면서도
천막처럼
햇살을 전깃불을 어둠을 가려주고 있다
가슴에 썩고 있는 나도
전신의 상처들이 들썩이며 모두 썩고 말았는지
움씰움씰 온몸이 가렵다 세상이 다 가렵다
방문을 걸어 잠그고 여덟 자 방 안
점점 늘어나는 벌레들
원형 탈모된 구멍마다 자리를 잡고 누웠을까
나의 생각의 움직임을 멈추고
그들이 부디 천천히 떠나가기를 기도한다

2

서재를 가득 메운
죽음의 향기마저 이제는 희미하다
여전히 사과 속에는 씨 하나 중심에 박혀 있다
중심의 씨방을 둘러싸고 일어서는
계곡과 완만한 언덕을 이루고 있는
과육의 박제된 견고한 겉껍질, 집착처럼
가파른 계곡 사이에 오솔길 끝에
낮은 지붕 하나 올린다
죽음이 충분히 즐기고 떠난 자리
시간은 제 관절을 마디마디 펴고
철탑처럼 일어섰다
길이 끝나는 으슥한 곳에
마른 향기로 지은 집 한 채 짱짱하게 완성되고
곳곳에 핀 곰팡이들이
장례식장 흰 국화처럼 얼굴을 들고
굳게 닫힌 방문을 지키고 있다
삼 년째 썩은 것들의 몸이
드디어 제법 단단하게 여물었다

About Rotting

1

The apple, rotted on the desk.
Maggots were swarming amid the pungent sweet smell.
In no time, the persistent movement
of them, sticking out their red bellies,
pushing forward with their plump bodies through the sweet liquid;
The next day, upon opening the door, at some point,
they spread their wings and take flight.
Sitting on the book, on the desk, on the piano,
is it already taking a rest, enjoying its leisure?
The apple, even as it fills its mushy body with maggots,
like a tent,
screens the sunlight, the electric lights, the darkness.
My heart rotting,
I wonder if all the wounds on my body have decayed.
I, too, feel itchy all over my body, and the world itches.
Within the small room with locked doors
the multiplying insects
have they settled in and lain on every circular, bald hole?
I stop the movements of my thoughts,

and I pray they leave slowly.

2

Filling the study,
even the scent of death has become faint.
Still, in the core of the apple, a single seed remains firmly.
Encircling and standing up around the central ovary,
The valley, and the stuffed hard shell of the sarcocarp,
forming gentle hills, like an obsession,
at the end of a path between the steep valleys,
a low roof has been raised.
Where death has sufficiently enjoyed and departed,
time stretches its joints, joint by joint,
standing up like a steel tower.
In the dreary place where the road ends,
a house built with dry scents is stoutly completed,
fungi blossoming in places,
raising their faces, like a white chrysanthemum at a funeral,
guard the firmly closed door.
The bodies, rotting for three years
have finally ripened solidly.

고사목 1

글렀어 다시 잎이 자라기에는
습관성 절망들 나이테 속으로 골똘히 스며든다
가지마다 귀버섯이 피고 이끼가 푸르다
글렀어 다시 잎이 자라기에는…….

무른 목질에 절망들 평화적으로 새겨질 때
바람도 멀리서 온도를 낮추며 온다
겨울을 향해 고독하게 서 있으면
병 없이도 순간 죽을 것 같다

신도시 아파트단지 잘 가꾸어진 화단에서
죽어가는 병은 나에게로만 스며든다
여러 종의 여러 그루의 나무 중에서
병이 나에게로만 스며드는 데는 이유가 있다

바람 앞에서 부러지고 건조되는
그 속에 든 평화에 나는 이미 길들여졌다
달콤한 병증에 중독된 나는
순순히 병을 받아들이는 자세를 고수한다

오래 묵은 병의 의지로 나는 선 채로 죽어간다

누구에게도 양도할 수 없는 이 의지는
가지 끝에서
죽음의 끝에서

다시 생으로 회류하는가
봄을 향해 서 있으면 허공들 몸살을 앓는다
먼 곳의 끝으로부터 물기가 돌기 시작한다

Dead Tree - 1

All is lost for leaves to grow again;
Habitual despair permeates deeply through the growth rings.
On each branch sprout mushrooms, and moss grows green.
All is lost for leaves to grow again…

As despair is peacefully engraved into the soft wood,
The wind, too, comes from afar, bringing a lower temperature.
Standing lonely towards winter,
I feel like dying soon without any illness.

In the well-tended flower bed of the new city's apartment complex,
The dying disease permeates only into me.
Among the many trees of various species,
There must be a reason why the disease seeps only into me.

I am already tamed by the peace in it
Which breaks and dries before the wind.
Addicted to the sweet symptoms of the disease,

I willingly maintain a posture of accepting the disease.

Under the will of the old illness, I am dying while standing;
This will, that cannot be transferred to anyone,
At the end of a branch,
At the end of death,

Do I return to life again?
Standing towards spring, the void suffers form aches;
Moisture begins to circulate from the end of the farthest.

고사목 2

새처럼 날고 싶다는 오래된 기도가
물관부마다 수문을 열어 놓는다
습관을 바꾸어 내부의 물기들
조금씩 몸 밖으로 내보낸다
내가 나를 돕지 않으면
누가 나를 돕겠는가
흔들리며 그림자 치수를 줄이는
겨울보다 몇 마디씩 희망을 낮추는 봄
흘러가며 스며들며 무너뜨리며
훼손된 나이테는 빙빙 회전만을 기억한다
살아있다는 감각이 도주로 막다른 곳처럼
뿌리 끝에서 흥건히 젖어 있다
물오른 나무들 앞 다투어 자라나는 곳에서
물에서 승하는 자 물에서 망하리니
내 뿌리들 유일하게 푹푹 썩어간다
썩은 잔뿌리까지
뿌리란 뿌리들 죄다 녹고 있다
날고 싶다는 집요한 기도는
소란스러운 햇빛 사이로 죽음의 등 뒤로
휘어지며 소스라치며 뻗어간다
응답하라 응답하라 오바

간절기의 화단 한 귀퉁이에서
이파리 죄다 떨어뜨리고
눈부신 빛을 뚫는 가지들
제각각의 방향으로 허공을 들어올린다

Dead Tree - 2

The old prayer for flying like a bird
Opens the sluice gates in every vein.
Changing my habits, I allow the moisture within
To release slowly from my body.
If I don't help myself,
Who will help me?
Spring that lowers hopes by a few degrees more than winter
While swaying, reduces the shadow's length.
Flowing, permeating, collapsing,
The growth rings damaged only remember spinning round and round.
The sensation of being alive,
Like a dead-end on the escape route, leaves my root tips soaked.
Where the water-saturated trees compete to grow,
One who thrives in water perishes in water.*
My roots are the only ones that are rotting;
Right down to the rotten fine roots,
All the roots are melting away.
The persistent prayer to fly
Twists and extends,

Screaming through the noisy sunlight and behind the back of death.

Answer, answer me, please!

In the corner of the changing seasons' flower bed of the,

Where all leaves are shed,

Branches pierce through the dazzling light,

Lift the void in their own directions.

2부
Part Ⅱ

고사목 3

가지마다 반짝이는 별을 바르고
아침을 맞이하면
나는 별의 지도가 된다

이런 날이면
나는 죽음 너머의 세계가
더욱 궁금해진다

너로부터 먼 곳에서
가지마다 별자리 이름을 갖고
나는 너의 울음을 닮아간다

네가 목 놓아 울고 떠난 이 땅에서
새들이 사라지고, 부은 발등 위로
길 고양이 한 마리 올라앉았다

네가 울고 있는 동안은
나의 가장 높은 곳이
너의 가장 낮은 곳이 되곤 한다

Dead Tree - 3

Putting twinkling stars on each branch
welcoming morning,
I become a map of the stars.

On such days,
I become more curious
about the world beyond death.

Far away from you,
holding a constellation's name on each branch,
I am beginning to resemble your weeping.

In this land where you once shed tears and departed,
birds disappear, and on the swollen instep
a street cat perches.

While you are crying,
the highest part of me
tends to be your lowest place.

고사목 4

바람의 의지에 따라 울음이 달라집니까

등이 휘도록 울 때마다
일찍이 멀어진 곳보다 더 먼 곳으로 쫓겨갑니까

누구의 명령으로 절망들 슬픔들 유전합니까

세상의 모든 관棺이 화려한 꽃들로 꾸며지듯이
가지마다 척척 별과 달이 꽂힙니까

날카롭게 반짝이는 어둠들 어둠이 만개하면
뒤늦게 돌아온 곳보다 더 가까이 돌아옵니까

구름들 바람들 고양이들 나에게 돌아옵니까

울음 하나로 가장 먼 곳까지 나아갔다가
가장 가까운 곳으로 돌아오는 나는 누구의 나입니까

Dead Tree - 4

Does the cry change depending upon the will of the wind?

Whenever I weep so sadly that I lose myself,
will I be chased to a place even further away than where I was once?

Who commands that these despairs and sorrows should be inherited?

As every coffin in the world is decorated with splendid flowers,
do stars and moons stick fast to each branch by themselves?

When the sharply sparkling darkness fully blooms,
does it return closer than the place it returned to late?

Will the clouds, the wind, and the cats return to me?

Who am I, who reaches the farthest place with a single cry,
and then returns to the closest?

손맛

백구의 목줄을 내게 쥐여주고
슬슬 잡아당기라고 아버지가 눈짓을 하였다
내 손 끝에 힘이 들어가고
오줌 얼룩이 든 마포 자루 속으로
두 눈 껌뻑이며 백구가 기어 들어갔다

댓잎 뒤척이는 소리에도
앞발을 치켜들고 커 엉 컹, 짖던
민감하게 짖던 그도
입가에 완벽한 체념을 물고,

백구의 목줄은
내 손 끝에서 수십 년을 떨고 있다
아무리 늙어도 손맛처럼 느껴지는 이 떨림
이 떨림 속으로,
아직도 나는 내 목줄을 따라다닌다

수완이 좋은 그는 어디에서
또, 뒷거래를 트고
슬슬 내 목줄을 당기는가 끈적거리는 손맛이 느껴진다

The Feeling of His Hand

Handing me the leash of Baekgu,
my father winked at me to pull it slowly.
My fingertips are tense
and into the sack with a pee stain
Baekgu crawled, blinking its eyes.

Even at the rustling sound of bamboo leaves,
raising its front paws and barking sharply,
barking sensitively,
he, with a complete sense of resignation on his lips,

The leash of Baekgu
has been trembling in my fingertips for decades.
This trembling sensation, as vivid as the feeling of a hand, no matter how old I become,
into this trembling,
still I follow my own leash.

Where is he, so resourceful,
opening a backdoor deal,

gently pulling on my leash? I can feel the sticky feeling of his hand.

손

형은 평생 독선생을 자청한
할아버지 두툼한 손을 가졌다
고등학교를 들어갈 나이가 되어서도
공책 몇 장씩 가족이름만을 필사하던
장애 이급의 손을 가졌다
그는 가난한 친구에게 할아버지 몰래
슬쩍 공책 몇 권 집어주던
날랜 손을 가지고 있다
대나무밭을 들락거리며
담배를 일찍 배우던
니코틴 노랗게 밴 손가락을 가졌다
구름 그늘 몇 근 내려앉을 때까지
어린 내가 꺽꺽 울면
말없이 내 등을 토닥여주던
골 붉은 손을 가지고 있다

그는 평생의 숙제처럼 적었던
鍾鍾. 賢賢. 貞貞. 容容. 이름자들
죄다 잊은 치매 깊은 손을 가지고 있다
내게는 그런 손을 가진 형이 있다

Hands

My brother's hands were thick like our grandfather's,
Who voluntarily became the sole teacher for him all his life;
Even when he reached the age to enter high school,
His hands were second-degree disabled,
Copying only family names in the notebooks.
His hands were nimble
That would secretly give away a few notebooks
To his poor friends without our grandfather knowing.
His hands were yellow with nicotine,
With which he would roam the bamboo groves
And learned to smoke at an early age.
His hands were red
Which silently patted my back
When I, a young child, cried
Until a few shades of cloud settled down.

His hands were of deep dementia, having forgotten
All the names he once wrote as a lifelong task:
Jong Jong, Hyun Hyun, Jeong Jeong, Yong Yong.
I have an older brother with such hands.

이름 하나 외우며

발가락에 자꾸 힘이 들어간다
보고 싶다 용아
땅바닥에 헌 운동화 끝으로
이름을 썼다 쓱쓱 지운다
정류장 한 귀퉁이 움푹 파이고
머리 위 백일홍 붉은 꽃이 흔들린다
꿈속에서도 올 수 없는
이승의 이정표 아래에서
지우지 못한 이름 하나 이렇게 외우며
나는 턱없이 늙어버린다
종점에서 종점으로 달리는 버스 안에서
장미꽃 울타리가 있는 붉은 지붕을
지나칠 때마다
손가락에 자꾸 힘이 들어간다
용아, 먼지 낀 유리창에 대고
지나가는 허공에 대고 너의 이름을
또박또박 눌러 쓴다
당신은 나를 알아보지 못하고
나는 당신을 알아보지 못하는
서로 낯선 얼굴이 되어서도
허공에서 사라지는 이름 한 송이

아직도 눈이 아프게 환하다

As I Remember a Name

My toes keep tensing up.
I miss you, Yong Ah
With my worn-out sneakers' tips on the ground,
I write your name and erase it.
A corner of the bus stop is deeply indented,
And the red flowers of the crape-myrtle tremble above my head.
Under the guidepost of this world,
Where I cannot come even in dreams,
Memorizing a name I can't erase,
I'm getting far too old.
In the bus traversing the country from end to end,
Every time I pass by the red-roofed house
With a rose-covered fence,
My fingers keep tensing up.
Yong Ah against the dust-covered window,
Against the passing air, I firmly write
Your name again and again.
You do no longer recognize me,
And I no longer recognize you.
Though we become strangers to each other,

A piece of your name that disappears into the air

Still remains so bright that it hurts my eyes.

온몸이 귀가 되어

아버지 집 대문 틈에 손수건 한 장 남몰래
끼워두고 돌아오던 길 나는,
꿈쩍 않는 높은 침묵을 따라
마을 끝 공동묘지까지 걸어간다
무덤과 무덤 사이에 더 작은 무덤 하나 베고
온몸을 지렁이처럼 끌어모은다
뗏장을 건들고 가던 바람이
섬뜩한 고요에 끼여 펄럭이는 소리
할미꽃이 허리를 곧추 세우는 소리
무덤과 무덤 사이를 건너다니는
흰나비의 날개 소리
작은 벌레들, 엉겅퀴 꽃에 붙어 말라죽는 소리
이마에 붉은 인장을 찍는 여름 볕의 발자국 소리
우물처럼 긴 두레박을 내려뜨리고
죽음과 죽음 사이에서 삭은 뼈를 길어올리는 소리
미나리 제비과의 묘화가 겹꽃을 펴는 소리
내 몸은 구멍마다 묘지의 소리로 채워지고
뒤늦게 저녁 짓는
어머니의 마른 솔가지 태우는 소리에
나는, 더럭 겁이 나서 몸을 일으킨다
죽음 위를 천천히 지나가는

어둠의 발자국 소리를 그믐달의 발자국 소리를
가만가만 세고 있는 커다란 귀 한 짝,
어둠을 털고 어슬렁어슬렁 공동묘지를 빠져나간다

Becoming All Ears

Sneaking a handkerchief into the gap in my father's house gate
And on the way back, I
Following a high and unwavering silence
Walk to the cemetery at the end of the village.
Lying on a grave smaller than the others,
I gather my body like an earthworm.
The sound of the wind fluttering,
Tangled in eerie tranquility
After toucheding the turf;
The sound of pasqueflowers straightening their backs,
The sound of white butterflies' wings crossing between graves,
The sound of small insects, drying up and dying, stuck to thistle flowers,
The sound of summer sun's footsteps stamping a red seal on our forehead,
Laying down a long bucket as one would into a well,
The sound of raising the bones decayed between death and death,
The sound of the buttercup opening its double flowers

Every hole in my body is filled with the sounds of the graveyard.

And late in the evening,

At the sound of my mother cooking over burning dry pine branches,

I, startled, lift my body.

A large ear, quietly counting

The footstep sounds of darkness and that of the waning moon,

Slowly passing over death,

Shake off the darkness and sneak out of the cemetery.

동치미

연탄불이 꺼진 성북동 월세방, 어디에도 연락이 닿지 않고 유리문을 두드리는 동지 바람소리가 요란하다 학력도 없는 형은 친구에게 빌려온 세계문고판 쿠오바디스를 겉장부터 찢어가며 '무소식이 희소식이여' 태평하게 딱지를 접는다 녹슨 주인집 철 대문을 돌멩이로 괴어 놓고 골목 끝까지 갔다 몇 번씩 돌아오는 사이 차박차박 달빛이 차오른다 삼 일째 가출중인 아우를 기다린다. 그늘진 곳에서 뚜껑이 닫힌 항아리 속, 삭힌 고추맛과 청강과 생강물이 배어드는 장물, 아직도 장맛이 너무 싱거워 장맛은 염도가 좌우한다며 내 生의 중심부에 한 주먹 소금을 풀어준다 두터운 몸속으로 차갑게 배어드는 간기 자연 숙성이 될 때까지 구름이 오락가락하는 성북동 언덕배기 그 집

Dongchimi*

In the monthly rental room in Seongbuk-dong, where the briquette stove has gone out, the sound of the wind, unable to find contact anywhere, loudly knocks on the glass door. My older brother, who has no educational background, tears away the cover of the World Library edition of Quo Vadis borrowed from a friend and leisurely folds flipping cards believing that 'no news is good news'. While he props open the rusted iron gate of the landlord's house with a stone and walks to the end of the alley and back several times, the moonlight fills the area with a rapid and firm pace. He waits for his younger brother, who has been running away for three days. In the shady area, inside a closed jar, the stored sauce flavored with fermented red pepper, sea mustard, and ginger water, is still too insipid. Saying that the sauce's flavor depends on the salinity, I add a fistful of salt into the core of my life; the house on the Seongbuk-dong hill where clouds come and go, letting the saltiness ferment naturally and seep coldly into my thick body.

*Dongchimi is a traditional Korean dish that is a type of kimchi. It is characterized by its watery, brine-like consistency and is made from radishes. Unlike the more familiar spicy red kimchi made with chili pepper flakes, dongchimi has a clear and refreshing broth, making it relatively mild in flavor.

추억도 문을 닫았다

삼홍 집 단골식당에 홀로 앉아
쓸쓸한 후회들이 빗물처럼
창틀에 고여 흘러넘치는 것을 본다
삼거리의 길이 녹는 동안
어둑한 들길 저 끝쯤에서
너희는 고양이 걸음으로 지나가는가
적막한 맘을 어둠에 비비며
내 속에서 새어나오는
작은 짐승들의 울음 같기도 한
가까운 인척들을 피해 다니는 오 년의 시간들
나는 말수가 부쩍 줄어들고
봄을 제일 많이 기다리는 사람이 되었다
가장 늦게 봄이 오는 이 길은
아는 사람은 단 한 명도 지나가지 않았다
농한기에 점심내기 화투판을 돌리던 이발소와
명절 떡을 쪄내던 삼거리 떡집만
빙그레 마주보고 문을 열고 있을 뿐
폐가 처분하는 가게들이 서로 마주보고
임대문의 딱지를 붙이고 있는
빈 유리창들뿐,
우리의 추억들도 죄다 문을 닫아걸었다

Memories Have Closed Their Doors

Sitting alone in the regular Samheung restaurant,
I see the lonely regrets, like rainwater
Pooling on the windowsill and overflowing.
While the streets at the three-forked junction melt away,
At the end of the dimming twilight path,
Are you passing by with the steps of a cat?
For five years of
Rubbing my desolate heart against darkness,
And avoiding the relatives
Who resemble the cries of small beasts
Leaking out from within me,
I have become less talkative,
And I wait for spring the most.
On this road, where spring arrives last,
Not a single person I know has passed by.
Only the barber shop that hosted card games during the slack season of farming
And the rice cake shop at the three-forked junction, steaming rice cakes for holidays,
Face each other smiling with open doors,
And the shops being cleared out are facing each other,

With empty windows

On to which 'For Lease' notices are stuck,

All our memories have also closed their doors.

작은어머니

아버지도 어머니도 죽어 나간 시골 집, 우리는 금기를 깨고 같은 자세로 누워 몇 눈금씩 키를 줄인다

마른 입술로 빽빽이 필사하는 폐가한 가문의 내력을 따라 그믐달은 궁금한 방향으로 몸을 옮기고, 아버지의 그, 여자는 딱딱한 등 뒤에서 쉴 새 없이 지난날을 반성한다

기억과 기억 사이로 수박 씨앗을 뱉어내듯 끊임없이 쏟아지는 말, 말의 호미질로 새삼 발굴되는 수장된 상처. 그녀와 나 사이에 눈에 보이지 않는 강 하나 흐르기 시작한다

담 밖 사람들에게는 말할 수 없던 시간을 슬쩍 건너 뛸 때마다 우리는 서로의 속으로 첨벙 물길을 트고 있다

첨벙첨벙 제 속으로 떨어지는 물소리에 취해서 쪽잠에 침몰하는 새벽녘, 다음 생엔 평생 너를 봉양하는 효성 깊은 딸로 내가 태어나마

약속인 듯 다짐인 듯 혼잣말을 되뇌이며 엄지손가락이 없는 손이 문득 내 손을 붙잡는다

Little Mother

In the countryside house, where both father and mother died, we break the taboo and lower ourselves by a few scales lying in the same posture;

Following the genealogy of our ruined family, we diligently copy with dry lips. Meanwhile the waning moon moves in a curious direction. Behind my father's stiff back, that woman, his lady, reflects incessantly on the past;

Words poured out incessantly like watermelon seeds spat out between memories, and newly unearthed water-buried wounds by the hoe of words. An invisible river starts to flow between her and me;

Whenever skipping over the times, we couldn't speak to those outside the walls, we splash into each other's hearts;

Intoxicated by the sound of water splashing into itself
And sinking into a dawn nap, I promise that in the next life I will be born as a dutiful daughter, caring for you throughout my life;

〉

Repeating this to herself, as if making a promise or a resolution, her hand without a thumb suddenly grips mine.

어떤 평화주의

남도창도 잘하고 학춤도 잘 추는
아버지는 사시사철 감수성이 풍부한 사내다
날씨에도 매우 민감한 사람이다

아버지는 중복 더위에
어머니의 턱을 어그러뜨려 놓고
보양식을 사먹으러 읍내로 나갔다

어머니는
얼굴을 가리고 손을 내젓고
나는 집을 뛰쳐나갔다

마을길을 피해 공동묘지 무덤들 사이에
웅크린 채, 별이 뜨는 것을 보았다
엄마가 부르러 오기를 기다리던 나날

겁 없이 잠들어 버리던 나날
무덤에 기대어 잠이 든 나는,
더 이상의 비극을 예상하지 않았다

A Certain Pacifism

My father, good at playing the Namdo-chang and dancing the Crane dance,
is a man of rich sensitivity in all seasons,
and of attuned to the changes in weather as well.

In the midsummer heat,
after breaking my mother's jaw,
he went into the town to eat nourishing food.

Mother,
covered her face, shaking her hand,
and I ran away from the house.

Avoiding the village road and crouching among the graves
in the public cemetery, I watched the stars rising.
The days when my mother would come to call me.

The days when I used to fall asleep without fear;
Leaning against one of the graves, I
did not anticipate any further tragedies.

실종

바람이 앞뒤로 분다
바람은 거대한 압축기다

사실처럼 집이 움직인다
사실처럼 집이 줄어든다

안이든 밖이든
바람의 세기는 종잡을 수가 없고
어느 날은 문짝을 괴어 놓는 것도
서로를 증명할 수가 없다

집은 닫혔다,
라는 동사의 묘한 영향력 안에 갇힌다
닫혔다 갇혔다 두 단어 사이에서
나는 줄곧 압축이 된다

물러난 벽이 물러난 벽의 등이 되었을 때
집의 무너짐은 서서히 믿음처럼
나를 먹어치운다
나는 사라진다, 연기처럼

이것은

누구에게나 일어날 수 있는 일이다

Disappearance

The wind blows back and forth;
The wind is a giant compressor.

Houses really seem to move;
Houses really seem to shrink.

Whether inside or out,
The wind's strength is unpredictable.
One day, the wind made the door closed,
Which can't prove each other.

I am trapped by the mysterious power of the verb:
The house is closed.
Between 'closed' and 'trapped,'
I am constantly compressed.

When a retreated wall becomes the back of another retreated wall,
The collapse of the house slowly eats me up
Like a belief.
I disappear, like smoke.

〉

This

Can happen to anyone.

小雪날 눈을 맞으며

암 치료를 포기하겠다는 아우를 돌려보내고 영통에서 동탄까지 눈을 맞으며 걸어갑니다

종로에서 성북동까지 비를 맞으며 걸었던 아득한 옛날처럼 왠지 살아서는 다시 못 볼 것 같은 얼굴 하나 어서 가라, 어서 가라, 小雪날 바람은 등 뒤에서 연신 등을 떠밉니다

신도시로 진입하는 능선 위에서 우뚝, 걸음을 멈추고 서 있는데 눈은 죽어라 죽어라 내립니다

가만히 뒤돌아보니 아우의 발자국도 내 발자국도 죄다 지워지고 말았습니다 이 길 위에는 우리가 만났다 헤어진 표식 하나가 없습니다

Catching Snowflakes on the Day of Minor Snow*

After sending my brother back, who decided to give up cancer treatment,

I am walking from Yeongtong to Dongtan in the snow.

Like the distant past when I walked in the rain from Jongno to Seongbuk-dong, a face that seemed like It would never seen again in life urges me, 'Hurry, go, hurry.' The wind on day with light snow continuously pushes my back.

Standing still on the ridge leading to the new city, the snow is falling like crazy.

When I quietly look back, the footprints of both my brother and me have been erased; On this road, there's not a single sign that we met and parted.

*Minor Snow : 20th of the 24 solar terms in East Asian lunisolar calendars, about late in November.

어떤 추억

할아버지는 큰아들인 내 아버지를 낳고 터 넓은 밭에 유실수를 심기 시작하셨단다. 학교에 입학할 때마다 한 그루씩, 군 입대를 할 때에도, 심지어 어머니와 혼인을 한 해에도 종이 다른 감나무를 심으셨단다. 유년시절 터 넓은 밭에는 죽은 큰오빠와 죽은 두 언니를 낳던 해에 심은 감나무도 해를 걸러 풍작이 들곤 했다. 대곡시, 광주골감, 봉화골감, 꾸리감, 평핵무, 개월하시 품종도 다양한 감나무들. 웬일인지 나무와 나무 사이가 좁혀질수록 아버지는 더욱 집 밖으로 돌고 할아버지의 긴 한숨은 깊어졌다.

할아버지 갑자기 숨 놓으실 때, 기다렸다는 듯이 집 밖에서 집터랑 한 묶음으로 밭문서를 넘기는 아버지. 그 해 가을도 못 넘기고 풋감 주렁주렁 매단 채 감나무들 뿌리째 뽑혀 나가는 것을 보았다. 내 감나무가 나무더미 밑에서 식은 땀 흘리는 것을 나는 온종일 본 적이 있다.

A Certain Memory

My grandfather, after my father, his eldest son, was born, began planting fruit trees in a large field. He planted different species of persimmon trees when his son entered school, enlisted in the army, and the year he married my mother. During my childhood, these persimmon trees in the large field planted in the years when my deceased elder brother and two sisters were born, yielded bountiful harvests biennially. The species included Daegoksi, Gwangjugolgam, Bonghwagolgam, Kkurigam, Pyeonghaekmu, Gaewolhasi. Strangely, the closer the distance between trees became, the more my father wandered out of the house, and the deeper my grandfather's long sighs became.

When my grandfather passed away suddenly, my father, as if having been waiting for the moment, handed over a bundle of the farm documents along with the house site outside the house. That year, even before autumn ended, I saw the persimmon trees, laden with unripe fruit, were uprooted. I have seen my persimmon tree sweating coldly all day under the pile of uprooted trees.

3부
Part Ⅲ

돌

내 책장에는 여러 개의 돌이 있습니다
볼프강에서 월악산 계곡에서
겨울바다에서 주워온 놈
부모님 산소 앞에서 반은 몸을 내놓고
반은 땅 속에 묻혀 있던 놈
그 중에서도, 마음이 먹먹할 때마다
나는 선산에서 가지고 온
구멍 많은 돌에게 자주 손이 갑니다
보리파종 적기인 상강에 이르면
구멍 난 그의 내력을 짚어보는
일이 유난히 잦아집니다
내 손이 자주 멈칫거리는 곳
그곳에는, 울지도 못하고 요양원으로 갔던
내 형이 늘 숨을 죽이고 숨어 있습니다
형은 나를 만날 때마다
번번이 참았던 울음을 터트리곤 합니다
그때마다 어떤 신호탄처럼
나도 기어이 참았던 울음을 터트립니다
우리 가족은 만날 때마다
시도 때도 없이 우는 구멍 많은 돌입니다

Stone

There are many stones in my bookshelf;

Those picked up from the Wolf river, from the valleys of Woraksan,

From the winter sea,

One half-exposed, half-buried

In front of my parents' grave.

Among them, when my heart feels down and gloomy,

I often reach for the porous stone

I brought from the family cemetery.

Around the time of Sanggang*, the optimal period for sowing barley,

I frequently contemplate the history of its holes.

In the holes where my hand often hesitates and halts,

My older brother, who went to the nursing home without crying,

Always hides, holding his breath.

Every time we meet,

He bursts into tears he always held back,

And then like some kind of signal,

I, too, inevitably burst into the held-back tears.

My family members are like a stone with many holes

Who cry incessantly whenever we meet.

*Sanggang : one of the 24 solar terms in East Asian lunisolar calendars, meaning "Frost's Descent" or "Descent of Frost" in English. This period typically falls around October 23rd each year. 'Sanggang' signifies the end of autumn and is considered an important point indicating the beginning of winter.

단단한 꽃

마음이 먹먹할 때마다
돌들의 무늬를 더듬어보던
내 손 끝에서
들숨일까 날숨일까
파르르 어떤 숨소리가 떨려옵니다
무늬에 따라서 일주일에 한 번
혹은 한 달에 한 번
꽃에 물을 주듯이
내 책장 위에 놓인 돌에게도
물을 주어야겠다는 생각이
그때 문득 들었습니다
처음에는 엉뚱한 생각을 한다고
스스로 도리질을 치곤 했지만
일주일에 한 번 혹은 한 달에 한 번
돌에게 물을 주기 시작하면서
돌이 피우는 꽃을
나는 황홀히 보곤 합니다
먹빛의 몸이 더 먹빛이 되어
베란다 한 귀퉁이에서
이읏고 숨 터지는 저 꽃들
오늘 다시 환하게 만개합니다

〉

당신 안에 살고 있는 돌 한 그루가

기어이 만개하는, 그날이 봄날입니다

Solid Flower

Whenever my heart feels down and gloomy,

From my fingertips,

Tracing the patterns of the stones,

A trembling breath, whether an inhalation or exhalation,

Comes fluttering.

Depending on the pattern, once a week,

Or once a month,

Like watering flowers,

Suddenly I thought

I should water the stones on my bookshelf.

At first, I shook my head

For the absurd thought,

But since I started watering the stones

Once a week or once a month,

I have ecstatically observed the flowers

They are blooming.

Those flowers, whose dark bodies become even darker,

Bursting out of breath at last

In the corner of the veranda,

Are blooming full bright again today.

The day when a stone living inside you
Finally blossoms, that day is spring.

즐거운 장례

요양원살이를 하던 오빠가
마침내 죽었다

강원도 주문진에 사는 맏누이와
경기도 동탄 수원 발안, 전라도 광주에 사는
남동생 넷과 여동생 넷
심지어 시애틀에 사는 동생까지
한밤중에 장례비 각출을 했다

다섯은 본명으로 그중 다섯은
이미 개명한 낯선 이름으로
'작은어머니' 통장에 숫자로 찍혔다
살아서 애물단지의 죽음이
뿔뿔이 흩어져 살던 핏줄들을
자석처럼 끌어당기고 있다

장례비는 오빠의 응급실 병원비부터
그리고 화장터 사용료와
꽃값 설렁탕 값 운구차 운임
운전기사 팁 식대까지
지불하고 지폐 몇 장 남았다

A Joyous Funeral

My older brother, who was staying in a nursing home,
Has passed away eventually.

The eldest sister living in Jumunjin, Gangwon-do,
Along with four brothers and four sisters
Living in Dongtan, Suwon, Balan in Gyeonggi-do, and Gwangju in Jeolla-do,
Even including my younger brother living in Seattle,
Contributed to the funeral expenses late into the night.

Five of them with their real names,
And another five with their newly changed, unfamiliar names,
Were listed as contributors in "the aunt's" bank account.
The death of a man, who was a trouble and strife while alive,
Was drawing the scattered bloodlines together like a magnet.

After paying my brother's emergency room hospital fees,
The crematorium fee,
The cost of flowers, Seolleongtang, the hearse fare,

Driver's tip and meals,

Only a few bills from condolence money remained.

꿈꾸는 자세

많이 그리우면 고향 쪽으로 얼굴을 돌리고 잔다

더 많이 그리워지면 그 꿈속에서도 얼굴을 돌리지 않는다

애벌레처럼 돌돌 몸을 말고 움직이지 않는다

The Posture of Dreaming

When I miss my hometown a lot, I turn my face towards it and sleep.

If I miss it even more, I don't turn away even in my dream;

Like a caterpillar, I roll up tightly and lie motionless.

피의 가계 1973

잦은 살생의 죄는 내게 물으시고 밀양 박씨 종부인 내 며느리 상한데 없이 죽음에서 벗어나게 하소서 원컨대 내 며느리 몸에 든 죽음을 작년에 죽은 박쥐에게 백년 전에 죽은 들쥐에게 나눠주소서

해 떨어지는 소리들 대나무 밭 가득 차오르면 할아버지는 깃발처럼 손을 번쩍 들어 올린다 단칼에 분리된 오리 몸통과 목 사이에서 분수처럼 솟는 따뜻한 피, 내가 들고 있는 막사발을 채운다 병이 깊은 엄마가 창백한 얼굴로 온몸을 부들부들 떨면서 막사발을 받아든다

동서남북 한 차례씩 절을 올린 할머니는 피 묻은 오리털로 며느리의 머리와 가슴과 얼굴과 등과 두 팔 마른 다리와 발등을 꼼꼼히 쓸어내린다 오리 몸통이 가마솥 안에서 끓는 동안 아궁이마다 장작 타는 소리들 요란하고 안방 구들장 데워지는 기운들 뒤란까지 훈훈하게 돌아간다

The Blood Lineage, 1973

I supplicate, blame me for the sin of frequent killing and let my daughter-in-law,

the chief wife of the Milyang Park clan, escape death unharmed;

I pray to Thee, God, to separate death from her and share it with the bat that died last year,

and the field mouse that died a hundred years ago.

As the sound of the setting sun fills the bamboo forest, my grandfather

abruptly raises his hands like a flag;

The warm blood spurting like a fountain between the separated duck torso and head,

fills the bowl I'm holding with jusr a stroke. My mother, severely ill, takes the bowl

with a pale face, trembling all over.

Grandmother, having bowed once toward all four directions, thoroughly wipes my daughter-in-law's head, chest, face, back, arms, lean legs, and the tops of her feet with the bloodied duck feathers. While the duck torso was boiling in the cauldron, the noisy sound of firewood burning in each A-gung-i* fills the air, and the energy warming the main room's ondol** spread warmly to the backyard.

*a traditional Korean hearth or stove used for heating and cooking. It is typically constructed as a part of the floor in traditional Korean houses, known as hanoks, and is connected to a system of underfloor heating called "ondol."

**it refers to the traditional Korean underfloor heating system, specifically the part that constitutes the heat-conducting floor structure in a room. It is an integral component of the "ondol" heating system, which is a unique and traditional Korean method of heating homes.

기울어지는 뼈

간혹 역전이나 네거리에서
귀신을 볼 줄 안다는 사람들이 있다
행인들 북적이는 틈바구니에서
자주 붙들려 듣는 저승의 안부들
내 정수리에 터 잡고 앉은 어머니
빽백처럼 매달려 있는 시아버지
허리춤에 전대처럼 묶인 시어머니
내 손을 꼭 붙들고 있는 할머니
생전에 한결같이
나를 지극정성으로 사랑해 주신 분들

나는 왕이 될 수 없을까 귀신의 왕
누구의 눈에도 보이지 않는 왕
어둠에서 어둠을 낳는 세습의 왕
어둠과 어둠을 이어주는 배달의 왕
어둠과 어둠으로 성을 쌓는 왕이 될 수 없을까
손등과 발등 죄다 저승꽃을 피우고
뼈를 기울이면, 저승의 왕이 될 수 있을까
나는 왕이 될 수 없을까
아무리 눈부신 태양이 떠올라도
눈뜨지 않는 어둠의 왕이 될 수 없을까

The Tilting Bones

Sometimes at the station or at the crossroads,
Some people claim to know how to see ghosts.
Among the bustling crowd of passers-by,
I, being stopped by them, heard the underworld greetings they spoke of.
My mother, perching on my crown,
My father-in-law, hanging like a backpack,
My mother-in-law, tied around my waist like a belt,
My grandmother, holding my hand tightly,
Those who loved me
With all their heart during their lifetime.

Can't I not become a king, the king of ghosts?
The king invisible to all,
The king of heredity who gives birth to darkness from darkness,
The king of delivery connecting darkness to darkness,
The king building a castle out of darkness,
And the king of the underworld
If I bloom underworld flowers on the backs of my hands and feet,

And if I tilt my bones, can I become the king of the underworld?

Can I not become a king,

No matter how dazzling the sun rises?

Can't I become the king of darkness who doesn't open his eyes?

검은 잉크

물이면서도 흐르지 못하는 죄목에 갇혔다
강줄기를 따라가거나 폭포수로 내려서 치거나
북극의 빙하로 얼어붙는 제 족속들과는
소식을 끊고 형벌처럼
한 가지 색으로만 짙어가는 시간 속에서
저 혼자 고였다 흘렀다 솟구쳤다
그 중 순한 속성 하나 붙잡고
기록하는 힘, 단 한 가지 색으로
융통성 없는 나는 바닥까지 내려가는 중이다
하지의 햇빛 한 올이나
그믐날 달빛 한 조각도 바람 반 토막도
뚜껑 안을 기웃거리다가 한 번 발목을 빠트리면
블랙홀처럼 천형 같은
암흑의 내면을 빠져나가지 못한다

밖에서 단색들을 움켜쥐고 너무 고독한 걸까
한 방울, 반말처럼 튕겨나가는 불손한 태도들을
그러니 가끔씩 용서해 주시라
계곡이나 강가에 줄지어 선 자작나무 사이를
흘러다니던 자유가
그들의 검은 내벽을 간혹 치는 모양이다

하늘의 일과 강줄기의 일에 더욱 몰두하는 요즘
다만 나는 나의 색을 내어주었을 뿐,
꼼꼼히 기록하는 일은 이제 그들의 뜻이 되었다

Black Ink

I am water, yet trapped in the crime of being unable to flow,

Cut off from my kin, who follow river currents, crash down waterfalls,

Or freeze into Arctic glaciers,

Like a punishment,

Alone, I pooled, flowed, and soared up.

In a time when it deepened into a single hue.

Clutching at one mild characteristic

With the power to record, with just one color,

Inflexible, I am sinking to the bottom.

Neither a ray of sunlight at the summer solstice

Nor a silver moonlight on the last day, not even a breath of wind can escape

If it slips its ankle while peeking beneath the lid,

It can't escape the darkness inside,

Like divine punishment akin to a black hole.

Am I too lonely outside, clutching monochromes tightly?

So, occasionally forgive me —

A drop of impertinent attitude that bounces off like informal speech.

The freedom that once flowed between rows of birch trees

By the valley or riverside

Seems to strike sometimes their black inner walls.

These days, absorbed much in the things of the sky and the rivers.

I merely gave away my color,

Now it became their will to keep meticulous records.

너에게 가는 길
— 선인장 뿌리

길은 사라진 지 오래다
눈 닿는 사방은 온통 모래뿐이다
건기의 막판에 이르러서는
그리움도 밑바닥에 닿았다
정말 아무도 그립지 않을 때
길 위에서 나의 그리움 하나
적막한 사막 안으로 내걸린다

아득히 절여오는 다리를 주무르는 밤에도
황량함과 조응하는 내 안에 무엇이 있어
나는 사막의 유목민이 되는가
더 이상 썩지 않는 몸
지상의 뿔처럼 가시들 짱짱해진다

사막뢰가 터질 때마다
가시와 가시 사이에 걸린 투명한 바람들
때때로 긴 목마름을 삼키며
나와 한 패거리가 된다
볼록한 바람의 힘으로
내가 다시 너에게 간다

오늘,

어둠 속 사막 안으로 곡선을 묻는 것은

나를 포기할 수 없는 나의 마지막 다짐이며

사막 안 모래 깊이 지주근을 내리고

완전한 어둠 속으로 들어서는 것은

너를 버릴 수 없는 내 운명 탓이다

The Way to You

— Cactus

The path has long since disappeared,

As far as the eye can see, there's nothing but endless sand.

At the end of the dry season,

My longing has also reached the bottom.

When I truly miss no one,

One of my longings still lingers on the path,

Hanging out in the desolate desert.

Even at nights when I massage my cramping legs,

Something within me corresponds to the desolation,

And will I become a nomad in the desert?

My body no longer decays.

Meanwhile, the thorns on the ground grow stronger, like horns.

Every time a desert thunder explodes,

The transparent winds caught between the thorns

Sometimes swallow long thirsts

And become one of my gangs.

With the power of the convex wind,

I go to you again.

〉

Today,

Burying a curve into the desert in the dark

Is my last commitment, unable to give up on myself,

Putting down struts deep into the sand in the desert

And stepping into complete darkness,

Is due to my fate, unable to abandon you.

빈센트 반 고흐

태초에 기도가 있었다
단란한 기도는
두 손목에 든 바람처럼
노랗게 붉어지곤 한다
교회는 변색되는 기도를
떠받들고 낡아가고
좁은 문을 뒤쪽에 열어둔 채
희미한 정신을 드높인다
주여, 당신 뜻대로 하소서!
오늘도 멀리 가지 못하고
휘파람은 교회 마당가를 맴돈다
해바라기들 노랑 속 회전율은
자잘한 돌 위에서 반짝인다
주운 돌멩이 하나 주머니에 넣고
기차가 떠나가는 역을 향해
너의 이름을 불러본다
하루가 느리게 지나간다
남은 귀 하나 허공에 걸어두고
새 울음을 모으는 시간
기차는 유배지를 찾아들 듯
어둠을 몰고 오고 있다

Vincent van Gogh

In the beginning, there was prayer.
A peaceful prayer,
Like wind held in both wrists,
Often turns yellow and red.
The church, holding up
The discoloring prayer, is getting old,
And leaving a narrow door open at the back,
Elevating a faint spirit.
Lord, let your will be done!
Today, too, not going far,
The whistle hovers around the churchyard.
The yellow sunflowers' rotation rate
Glitters on tiny stones.
Putting a picked-up pebble in my pocket,
Towards the station where the train leaves
I call out your name.
The day goes by slowly.
With the remaining ear hanging in the air,
A time to gather bird songs,
The train, as if seeking a place of exile,
Is bringing darkness.

성 폴 요양소* 앞에서

나의 희망으로 나는 여기까지 왔다
지극한 슬픔들을 이렇게 묻는다
소란에서 소란으로 소음에서 소음으로
고요에서 고요로 적막에서 적막으로

너와 내가 마주 섰을 때
서서히 일어서는 벽
너와 나 사이 동서로 길게 뻗은 회색 벽 속에는
상처 많은 짐승 한 마리 살고 있다

벽의 균열 속으로 꾸역꾸역
지금껏 걸었던 내 길들을 풀어놓으면
날카로운 늑대의 울음들
수직으로 자라나고
내벽을 후비며 차곡차곡 어둠이 된다

벽은 욱신거리는 울음의 탄력으로
저렇듯 높고 단단해졌다
남프랑스의 새들, 내 파르스름한 입술과
초췌한 빰 위에서 맴돌고 있을 때

슬그머니 벽에 기대어 있으면
땅이 벽을 들어올린 듯
벽 틈바구니가 열리고 늑대의 울음소리들 밖으로 튀어나온다
데굴데굴 겨울나무 사이로 굴러가는 것이다

누구의 희망으로 나는 이곳까지 왔을까
나의 일기는 변명 없이 끝났다
지금부터의 나의 기록은 일기장 밖의 일기들
소란에서 멀리 소음에서 멀리

*생 레미 프로방스에 있는 생 폴 드 모졸 수용소 요양소. 아를에서 25km 떨어진 곳에 있다. 고흐는 스스로 들어와 가장 고통스러운 시기에 수많은 명화를 남겼다.

In Front of the Saint Paul Asylum*

With my hope, I have come here.
I bury such extreme sorrows
from turmoil to turmoil, from noise to noise,
from silence to silence, from desolation to desolation.

When you and I stood face to face,
a wall slowly rising
between you and me, in this long grey wall stretching east to west,
a beast lives with many wounds.

Into the cracks in the wall, laboriously,
if I let go of the paths I've walked till now,
the sharp cries of wolves
rise vertically,
and scratching the inner walls, gradually become darkness.

The wall has grown high and solid,
with the elasticity of throbbing cries.
When the birds of Southern France hover
over my pale lips and gaunt cheeks.

〉

If I lean slowly against the wall,
as if the earth has lifted the wall,
a gap in the wall opens and the cries of wolves leap out of it,
rolling between the winter trees.

With whose hope did I come this far?
My diary ended without excuses.
My records from now on are diaries outside the diary,
far from turmoil, far from noise.

*Located in Saint Remy de Provence, the Saint Paul de Mausole asylum is 25 km away from Arles. Van Gogh voluntarily admitted himself there and, during his most painful period, left behind many of his masterpieces.

오베르의 교회 먼지 희뿌연 방명록에

사랑이 그대의 손에서 시작되었다면
우리의 사랑은 그대의 손에서 자랐을 것이다

어둑한 교회 제단에
촛불을 켜고
두툼한 방명록에
누런 종이 위에
우리의 만남과 결별은
그대의 손에서 운명을 다하였다고 쓰고는

새들이 떠나간 밀밭을
멍한 표정으로 돌아보는데
신자 한 명 없는 시간 뒤에서
누군가 소리 죽여 울먹인다

하늘이 없는 것 같은
높은 천장을 올려다보며
1월의 나도
소리죽여 한참을 울었지만
울음의 이유를
한 마디도 묻지 않고 스쳐간 이神가 있다

〉
(만일 우리가 다시 만난다면 무슨 말을 할까요)

참 멀고도 높은 오베르의 교회
먼지 희뿌연 방명록에는
어느 기록물법에도
저촉되지 않는 내생來生의 선약이 젖어 있다

In the Dusty, Faint Guestbook of the Church in Auvers

If love began in your hands,
our love would have flourished there.

At the dim altar of the church,
lighting a candle,
on the thick guestbook,
upon the yellowed paper,
writing that our meeting and parting
fulfilled their destiny in your hands,

Looking back with a dazed expression
at the wheat field abandoned by the birds,
behind the time without a single believer,
someone's sobbing quietly.

Looking up at the high ceiling
that seems without a sky,
I too, in January,
cried quietly for a long while,
but there is a god who passed by
without asking a single word about

the reason for the tears.

(If we would meet again, what would we say?)

The church of Auvers, so distant and lofty,
in its dusty, faint guestbook,
is soaked with a prior commitment from my forthcoming life,
violating no archival law.

카리카손의 밤에 쓴 엽서

이곳에서는 내 식으로 창을 낼게요

당신과 나 단둘이 작은 벽난로 앞에 앉아
마른 장작 하나둘 집어넣어가면서 화기를 조절해요
안락의자 두 개 놓인 거실에는 커튼 하나 달지 않고

잠든 시간 깨어 있는 시간 구분하지 말고 정원의 새소리를 들어요

아프게 서로 짓찧었던 부위마다 붉은 약 발라주며 미안하다 후후 서로 용서해요

한 사람이 죽으면 다른 한 사람이 나중 죽을 때까지

소식하는 당신 식성을 따라 채식菜食으로 아침을 먹어요

천천히 그렇게 손잡고 마침내는 함께 죽어요

중천에 환하게 뜬 달 마당 한가운데 연못에 걸려 멈춰 있는 이곳은 프랑스 남부의 카리카손이에요

소박하지만 예의가 바른 뭇 사람들이 돕고 사는 마을 따사로운 햇

빛 한 오라기 어깨에 걸치고 바람소리 환하게 들리는 우리의 출생지 같은 이 마을 곳곳 동네 길을 다 걸어서 길 끝까지 걸어서 마을 뒷길 수많은 텃밭 중 가장 경사진 땅 몇 평쯤 세를 얻고요

두렁마다 종을 바꾸어 씨를 뿌려요 치커리 당근 방울토마토 상추 열무 배추랑 절기에 따라 푸릇푸릇 솎아내는 일

새벽잠 줄이고 뒤늦은 농사법 천천히 배워갈까요?

나의 초대를 곧 수락해 주세요

이 엽서를 받을 수 있는 주소를 부디 내게 보내주세요

Postcard Written on a Night in Carcassonne

Here, I'll make a window in my own way.

You and I, sitting alone in front of a small fireplace,
adjust the fire by adding one log then another,
We do not hang a single curtain in the living room, which has two armchairs.

Both in sleeping time and waking time, let's listen to the birds in the garden.

we apply red medicine to the spots where we hurt each other, say "I'm sorry", and forgive each other with a breath.

If one of us dies, until the other shall die later

Following one's dietary habits, the other would eat vegetarian meals for breakfast.

Holding hands, slowly, we finally die together.

This is Caricason in southern France, where in the middle of the sky, the moon, hanging over the pond in the center of the yard, brightly shines.

A village where modest yet courteous people live and help each other, with a ray of warm sunlight on our shoulders, like our birthplace, with the sound of wind clearly heard, walking through every street in the village to the end of the road, renting a few patches of the steepest land among numerous vegetable gardens.

Let's sow seeds by changing the species in each ridge; chicory, carrots, cherry tomatoes, lettuce, summer radishes, and cabbages, which we will pluck fresh according to the season.

Shall we reduce sleep in the morning and slowly learn the belated farming?

Please accept my invitation soon.

Please send me the address where you can receive this postcard.

아무르 강가에서

여기는 두 개의 시계가 있다
너는 북쪽의 시계를 나는 남쪽의 시계를 본다
흐린 강물을 따라 철새를 따라
시간은 습지의 향을 맡으며 북쪽으로 흘러간다
우리는 눈을 감고 휘파람을 불었다

새들의 합창소리를 따라
너의 시계는
늘 나의 시계를 앞서 간다
조율을 맞춘 피아노 검은 건반처럼
새들은 붉은 허공에 박혀 울고

낮은 언덕을 오르면
강물은 무덤이 된다
노을들 솔솔 같은 음을 반복하며
허공을 무너뜨린다
점점 붉어지는 강물들

마당이 없는 곳에서 새들은 또 태어나고
우리의 슬픔에는 계절이 없다
우리의 이별에는 아무런 이유가 없다

북쪽은 북쪽의 시계를 보고
남쪽은 남쪽의 시계를 보고 앞으로 나아간다

무덤이 없는 곳에서
새들은 죽음을 맞이하고
먼 곳에서 나는
먼 곳에 있는 너를 생각하고 있었다

By the Amur River

Here, there are two clocks.

You watch the clock of the north; I watch the clock of the south.

Following the cloudy river, following the migratory birds,

Time flows northward, smelling the scent of the marsh.

We closed our eyes and whistled.

Following the chorus of birds,

Your clock

Always runs ahead of mine.

Like the black keys of a tuned piano,

Birds embed themselves in the red air and cry.

Climbing a low hill,

The river becomes a grave.

Repeating a rustling tune,

The sunsets collapse the sky.

The rivers are getting redder.

In a place without yards, birds are born anew.

Our sorrow knows no reason,

Our parting has no reason.

The North looks at the clock of the North,

The South looks at the clock of the South and moves forward.

In a place where there are no graves,

Birds face death,

And from afar, I was

Thinking of you, who were also far away.

4부
Part Ⅳ

알혼 섬에서 쓴 엽서

잊겠다는 결심은 또 거짓 맹세가 되었다

시베리아행 기차의 차창 밖으로 던진 익숙한 이름 하나
섬에 도착하니 환한 밤에 별들로 떠 있다

푸른색이 선명한 엽서의 뒷면에 가까운 곳이라고 쓰고 그 아래 아득한 곳이라고 쓴다

오물이라는 생선을 끼니마다 먹는다고 쓰고
꽁치와 고등어의 중간 종(種)인 것 같다고 덧붙인다

엽서보다 내가 더 먼저 도착할지 모른다고 쓰고
수영장 의자에 길게 드러누워 눈을 감는다

풀밭에 앉아 네잎크로버를 찾는 사람
푸른 호수로 내려가는 사람
전망대로 올라가는 사람
길의 방향은 각각 다르지만 영혼의 처소(處所)도 다른 사람

해가 지지 않는 저녁
검은 선글라스를 쓰고

입으로만 웃음을 보이고
밥을 먹고 차를 마시고 보드카를 마시는 일
이 낯선 동화의 나라에 기적처럼 와서
꿈같은 현실이라고

잠은 쏟아져도 말은 줄어들지 않는 시간
이 아름다운 순간을 침묵할 수는 없어서
노란색 꽃을 꺾어 바이칼 호수 지도 사이에 넣고 다닌다고 쓴다

아프고 아픈 손, 그 손으로 쓰고 또 쓴다
눈물 없이도 나는 너에게 전할 소식이 있는 것이다

Postcard Written from Olkhon Island

The resolution to forget has again become a false vow.
A familiar name, thrown out of the window of the train to Siberia,
When I arrive at the island, it is floating with the stars in the bright night.

On the vivid blue back of the postcard I write that it's a nearby place,
And beneath it, add it's a distant place.

I write that I eat a fish called Omul* at every meal,
Adding that it seems to be a species between saury and mackerel.

I write that I may arrive earlier than the postcard,
And then lie stretched out on a pool chair, closing my eyes.

People sitting on the grass, looking for a four-leaf clover,
walking down to the blue lake,
and going up to the observatory
whose directions of paths are different, as are the dwellings

of souls.

In the evening when the sun never sets,
wearing black sunglasses,
smiling only with mouth,
eating,
drinking tea,
and drinking vodka;
it's a dreamlike reality
in this unfamiliar land of fairy tales.

The time when even if I fall alseep, words never become fewer.
I cannot keep silent during this beautiful moment,
so I write that I pick yellow flowers and place them between the pages of the map of Lake Baikal.

With a hand that hurts and aches, I write and write again.
Without tears, I still have news to say to you.

*Omul – also known as Baikal omul is a whitefish species of the salmon family endemic to Lake Baikal in Siberia, Russia.(from wikipedia)

경사지에서 온 편지

라라, 인적이 뜸한 숲에서 나는 고양이와 단둘이 살고 있어 나무와 나무사이가 촘촘한 이 숲 속에는 나무의 그늘이 두터워서 나무와 그림자를 구분할 수가 없지

나뭇잎들 땅을 양탄자처럼 덮고 있어서
그 아래 식물들이 자라나기도 하지
땅에 몸을 엎드리고 손을 뻗어 오직 촉감으로
촉각으로 라라의 안부를 더듬거릴 때가 있지

손에 닿을 듯 말 듯한 거리에서 툭 툭 툭, 겨울비가 내리고 있어 빛을 좋아하는 생물종은 죽고 땅이 서서히 무너지고 있는 것만 같아

나의 고양이는 어둠의 채집자이자
열의를 가지고 살아가는 아마추어 로맨티스트야

그는 내가 준 밥에 의지하여 명랑하게 놀고 수시로 숙면을 취하거든, 매일 지속적으로 꼬리를 들고 돌참나무 소나무 활엽수 군락을 횡단하고 돌아오곤 해, 가끔씩 은혜 갚은 호랑이처럼 죽은 쥐를 물고 와서 풀 위에 놓곤 하지

가만, 나는 고양이와 단둘이 살고 있는 게 아니었어

죽은 쥐들과도 함께 살고 있다고 고쳐 쓸게

Letter from a Slope

Lara, I live alone with a cat in a deserted forest. The woods are dense and the shadows of the trees are so thick, it's impossible to distinguish between the trees and their shadows.

The leaves are covering the ground like a carpet,
and beneath them, plants grow.
Sometimes, I bow down on the earth, stretching out my hand,
guided only by my sense of touch,
groping for Lara's well-being through touch alone.

At a distance that seems almost within reach, pat, pat, pat, winter rain is falling. It feels as if light-loving species are perishing and the ground beneath is slowly collapsing.

My cat is a hunter of darkness,
An amateur romantic living zealously.

He frolics in good spirits eating the food I give him, sleeps soundly when he feels like it, twirling his tail, crossing groves of oaks, pines, and broad-leaved trees, returning every day, and sometimes, like a tiger repaying a favor, and he brings a dead mouse and places it on the grass.

Wait, I think I'm not living alone with just my cat.
I should rewrite: I live with dead rats, too.

루마니아의 여름

손에 든 아이스크림처럼 녹아 흐르고 있었다

들끓는 거리에서 원숭이는
사람처럼
귀를 쫑긋하고 앉아서
인간의 소원을 듣고 싶어 했다

동물 조각상 앞에서 예기치 않게 남의 소원을 엿듣고 말았다

누군가의 유배지에서
말하지 않으면 죽을 것 같은 말들이
끝내 터져 나올까 봐,
입술을 자근자근 깨물고 깨물었지만
갑자기 마른기침이 터졌다

그대에게 들려주고 싶었던 소원을 원숭이에게 모두 말해버렸다
원숭이 귓구멍이 팽팽해졌다
여행은 줄곧 걷는 일,
여행이 절반쯤 지나고 체중이 줄어들었다

두 귀가 줄곧 붉어졌다

검은 양산으로 높은 태양을 가리고
자유 시간 내내 걸었다

The Summer in Romania

It was melting and flowing like the ice cream in my hand;

On the sweltering streets, a monkey sat
with its ears pricked up like a person,
eager to hear the wishes of people.

Unexpectedly, I overheard another person's wish in front of an animal statue.

In someone's place of exile,
fearing the words that I was eager to burst out
would burst out at last,
I repeatedly bit my lip to hold them back,
but suddenly, a dry cough broke out.

I told the monkey all the wishes I wanted to share with you.
The monkey's ear holes perked up;
Travel is all about walking;
After about halfway through the journey, I lost weight.

My ears have turned red all the time;

Shielding myself from the high sun with a black parasol,
I walked throughout my free time.

코카서스의 밤

나의 숙소는 넓은 창문을 열면 설산을 향해 있다
자정 무렵 어둠속 달을 따라
가파른 산등성이에 시선을 올려두고
나는 희디흰 눈(雪)이 쌓인 추위를 가슴에 올려둔다
내 룸메이트는 이상하게 생각할 새벽이 가까워지는 시간
내 안에서 일어나는 눈사람,
아직도 나는 추위에 약한 두 눈이 큰 겁 많은 소녀다
분명 우리는
어느 기차역 계단에서 이야기를 나눈 적이 있다
높은 난간에 서서 오른쪽 발을 허공으로 떨어뜨리던
광대뼈가 도드라진 얼굴 하나,
녹아가며 추락하는 눈 코 입 희미한 미소
전쟁의 밤을 뚫고,
달빛이 내 방으로 여름 눈(雪)을 짊어지고 오고 있다

The Night in Caucasus

My accommodation faces the snow-capped mountains when I open the wide window.

Around midnight, following the moon in the darkness,

I lift my gaze to the steep mountain ridge,

And I bear the cold of the white snow on my chest.

As dawn approaches, when my roommate might think it queer,

A snowman arises within me,

Still, I am a scared girl with large eyes, vulnerable to the cold.

Surely we have

Once exchanged words on the stairs of some train station.

Standing on a high railing, dropping the right foot into the void,

A face with prominent cheekbones,

And with melting feathres—nose, lips, mouth—and a faint smile

Through the the war-filled night,

Moonlight shoulders the summer snow into my room.

백지의 계절에

조지아, 트빌리시에는 절벽 위에 아슬아슬한 터에 집을 짓고 사는 사람들이 있다고 편지를 쓰기 시작했다

높은 마당가에서 건조되는 빨래들을 올려다보며 잠깐 더위를 잊을 수 있는 이 도시가 좋다고

밤마다 아슬아슬하게 열린 높은 곳의 창문을 통해 지상의 안부를 묻는 별처럼, 그대는 멀리에 있는 나를 생각하면 이렇듯 더운 날씨의 변화에도 걱정이 많은 것 같다고 쓴다

아 덥다 더워, 왜 이렇게 덥지? 사는 게, 어디든 똑 같나 봐. 오후 관광은 박물관에서 도시의 가장 높은 곳으로 옮겨갔다고

가장 높은 곳에 있는 교회와 어머니 동상 주위를 한 바퀴 돌고 왔다고 경사진 길 위에서 별과 달의 관점에서 보는 지상의 안부들 꼼꼼하게 적는 일, 이것은 우리의 습관인 것 같다고

여기의 길은 등을 떠밀면서 서로를 박박 지워내는 백지의 계절이라고 마지막 문장을 쓰고 있다

In the Season of Blank Paper

I began writing letters mentioning that in Tbilisi, Georgia, there are people who build their houses perilously on the top of cliff;

And that I like this city where I can forget the heat for a moment, looking up at the laundry drying in the high courtyards;

I write every night, like a star inquiring about the earth's well-being through a dangerously open high-rise window, when you think of me from afar, you seem to worry about me a lot, even with the changes in the hot weather.

And I write that ah, it's hot, so hot! why is it so hot? Life might seem the same everywhere, and that the afternoon tour moved from the museum to the the city's highest part;

And that we took a walk around the church and the statue of the mother at the highest point, and that writing down meticulously the world's well-being from the stars' and moon's perspective of on the inclined roadhas become our habit;

〉

And in my last sentence, I write that the road here is a season of blank paper, erasing each other as the push against each other's backs.

숲길

빈 요구르트 병, 커피를 나눠 마신 듯한 종이컵,
투명한 생수병,
이슬에 젖은 담배갑,

숲에 떨어진 아주 적은 양의 쓰레기는 그루터기들로 이어진다

당신이 지나간 흔적이다

나는 당신이 지나간 흔적을 따라가고 있다

Forest Path

Empty yogurt bottles, paper cups shared for coffee,
Transparent water bottles,
Dew-soaked packs of cigarettes,

The very small amount of trash fallen in the forest leads to the stumps

These are the traces of your passing

I am following the traces you've left behind.

소나무

내 이야기는 기후와 땅에서 시작되지

나는 추운 고원지대, 거의 사막화된 곳,
모래와 자갈 지대에서 잘 자라지

사람들이 모두 떠나버린 뒤,
나는 그 땅을 차지하지
나는 화산이 분출하거나 빙하가 움직일 때
바람과 바다가 모래 퇴적을 일으킬 때
처음으로 그곳에 뿌리를 내리는 식물이지

나는 적막과의
마주침을 통해서만 번창하지

인간, 송이버섯, 내가 숲을 창조하는 역사의
각각의 숲,

나는 적막의 그림자를 통해 모습을 보이지
나의 이름을 통해 계절을 보이기도 하지

Pine Tree

My story begins with the climate and the land

I grow well in cold highlands, nearly desert-like places,
And in sandy, gravelly areas.

After everyone has left,
I take the land;
I am the first plant to take root there
When volcanoes erupt or glaciers move,
When wind and sea cause sand deposits,

I flourish
Only through encounters with desolateness.

Humans, pine mushrooms, each forest
In the history of creating forests,

I reveal myself through the shadow of desolateness,
And I show the seasons through my name.

상강

내가 서울로 떠날 때, 할머니는

마을회관 앞 정류장까지 배웅 나오셨다

시월 북풍에 파랗게 익었던 하늘

김장배추 포기마다 푸릇푸릇 흡입되고

동쪽 하늘 낮달

무밭 두렁마다 사각사각 서리로 내린다

Sanggang*

When I leave for Seoul, my grandmother

Came out to see me off at the bus stop in front of the village hall.

The sky ripened to blue under the north wind of October

Was vividly absorbsed by single piece of kimchi cabbage, green and lush,

A daytime moon in the eastern sky,

Crunch by crunch, descends upon each ridge of the radish field as frost.

*Sanggang : one of the 24 solar terms in East Asian lunisolar calendars, meaning "Frost's Descent" or "Descent of Frost" in English. This period typically falls around October 23rd each year. 'Sanggang' signifies the end of autumn and is considered an important point indicating the beginning of winter.

조지아에서 아르메니아로 넘어가는 국경지대

여권을 펼쳐들고 선 채 부고를 받았다
죽지 않고 버티는 방법에 골몰하던
국경의 태양이 온몸으로 소리치며
쓰러지듯 덮쳐 왔다. 전쟁이 한창인 7월,
울음을 터트리기도 전에 울음이 멈춰지고
국경 하늘은 피로 물든 흰 손수건처럼 펄럭이고
바람들 새들 입을 틀어막은 듯
사방이 정적에 들었다,
아스라이 잠잠해지는 두 귀
달궈진 울음이 내 몸 밖으로 뛰쳐나가
비척비척 국경을 넘어서는데
묘한 생명력이 '속울음' 을 닫지 못한다
울음을 줄줄 흘리며 낯선 곳으로 이동하는 몸

In The Border Area from Georgia to Armenia

I received the news of his death while standing with my passport open.

Engrossed in figuring out how to survive without dying,

The sun at the border screamed with its entire body

And came crashing down as if it were collapsing. In July, at the height of the war,

I stopped myself from crying before I could even start,

And the border sky fluttered like a blood-stained white handkerchief,

Silence fell all around,

As if it had muzzled the winds and birds,

My ears faintly grew quiet,

A heated cry burst from my body,

Shuffling across the border,

A strange life force is unable to silence the 'internal cries'.

A body moving to a strange place, continuously shedding tears.

해설

내생(來生)의 기록을 향해

— 박소원의 시

박덕규(시인, 문학평론가)

1. '왜 쓰는가'를 물으며

왜 쓰는가, 하고 묻는다. 쓰는 사람에게도 묻고, 쓰려는 사람에게도 묻는다. 쓰는 사람도 묻고, 쓰려는 사람도 묻는다. 대답은 많고, 많았지만, 대답하지 않은 사람도, 나아가 대답한 사람도 묻는다. 묻고, 또 묻는다. 왜 쓰는가? 박소원이 묻는다. 아니, 박소원에게 묻고 싶다. 왜 쓰는가?

2004년에 문단에 나온 박소원은 지금까지 『슬픔만큼 따뜻한 기억이 있을까』(2010), 『취호공원에서 쓴 엽서』(2013), 『즐거운 장례』(2021) 등 시집 세 권을 냈다. 시집에 넣지 않은 시들도 꽤 된다. 그러고도 쓴다. 시인이면 쓰는 사람이고, 시집 세 권은 이즈음 시를 쓰고 있는 시인이라면 대체로 생전에 가닿을 수 있는 수량이기는 하지만, 그래도 박소원에게는 묻고 싶어진다. 왜 쓰는가? 박소원도 묻고 있다. 왜 쓰는가? 그리고 스스로 대답도 한다.

잊겠다는 결심은 또 거짓 맹세가 되었다

시베리아행 기차의 차창 밖으로 던진 익숙한 이름 하나
섬에 도착하니 환한 밤에 별들로 떠 있다

푸른색이 선명한 엽서의 뒷면에 가까운 곳이라고 쓰고 그 아래 아득한 곳이라고 쓴다

오물이라는 생선을 끼니마다 먹는다고 쓰고
꽁치와 고등어의 중간 종(種)인 것 같다고 덧붙인다

엽서보다 내가 더 먼저 도착할지 모른다고 쓰고
수영장 의자에 길게 드러누워 눈을 감는다

풀밭에 앉아 네잎크로버를 찾는 사람
푸른 호수로 내려가는 사람
전망대로 올라가는 사람
길의 방향은 각각 다르지만 영혼의 처소(處所)도 다른 사람

해가 지지 않는 저녁
검은 선글라스를 쓰고
입으로만 웃음을 보이고
밥을 먹고
차를 마시고

보드카를 마시는 일
이 낯선 동화의 나라에 기적처럼 와서
꿈같은 현실이라고

잠은 쏟아져도 말은 줄어들지 않는 시간
이 아름다운 순간을 침묵할 수는 없어서
노란색 꽃을 꺾어 바이칼 호수 지도 사이에 넣고 다닌다고 쓴다

아프고 아픈 손, 그 손으로 쓰고 또 쓴다
눈물 없이도 나는 너에게 전할 소식이 있는 것이다

—「알혼 섬에서 쓴 엽서」 전문

박소원 시의 '쓰기' 문제는 주로 편지나 일기 등 '나'가 직접 기록하는 것과 관련해 드러난다. 위 대목에서 '나'는 엽서를 쓰고 있다. 그것은 당연하게도 엽서의 수신자인 '너'에게 '전할 소식'이 있어서다. 그런데 여기서 '엽서를 쓴다'는 건 실제 쓰고 있는 행위를 말하는 게 아니라 이 시 자체, 시를 쓰고 있는 자체로서의 '엽서 쓰기'를 뜻한다. '전할 소식'이란 것도 멀리 와 있는 '나'가 '아픈 손이 더 아파지면서까지 직접 쓴 편지를 발송해서 소식을 전하는 것'일 수 없다. 즉, 편지(엽서)로 '전할 소식'이란 바로 이 시 내면의 '나-화자'와 '너-시적 청자'의 관계에서의 '발화 내용', 그것의 기표/기의인 것이다. 시는 원래 기표를 통해 기의를 이해하는 과정으로 가치를 생성하는 장르인바, 박소원의 많은 시는 '쓰기'라는 행위를 '기표'를 내세워 그것을 통해 그 '쓰기'의 목적인 '전할 소식으로서의 기의'를 부각하는 과정을 내재하고 있다. 간단히 줄이면 이 시는

'아프게 써서 전달하는 소식' 을 드러내려는 것이 아니라 '아프게 쓰고 있는 그 자체' 를 드러낸 거다. 시에 나오는 '시베리아 기차', '푸른 호수', '알혼 섬', '전망대' 등은 시의 공간적 배경이자 '나-화자' 가 발화하는 실제 장소로서 그 '아픈 분위기' 의 실감을 배가하는 데 일조한다.

2. 존재론-자기성찰

박소원 시가 '왜 쓰는가' 를 자문(自問)하고 그것에 대해 자답(自答)하는 과정을 드러낸다는 사실은 실제 쓴다는 사실을 기표로 한 위와 같은 경우 말고 다른 시에서도 어렵지 않게 확인할 수 있다.

> 나뭇가지와 가지의 틈새와 끼어
> 마음과 마음을 미닫이창처럼 여닫고 앉아서
> 한 시절을 통째로 보내었다
> 매 앰 매 앰 매 애 앰
> 발음막이 터지도록 무시로
> 낯선 소리가 줄줄 새는 몸의 균열을
> 들여다보면서
> 오늘도 울음으로 살아내는 법을
> 한 마디씩 배우고 있다
> 삶의 본능처럼 작동되는
> 울음의 센서가 몸과 연결되어 움직이는 것을
> 혼자서 조용히 감지할 뿐,
> 낮에는 나무껍질 밑에 숨어 있다가

밤이 되면 튀어나오는 수상한 울음소리들

실은 나를 다 털어서 걸고 하는

절박한 게임이라는 것을 눈치 채는 이는 아무도 없다

자신을 다 걸고 덤벼들어도

고작 하루를 살아내는 일이어서야

쯧쯧쯧, 도박 치고는 스스로에게 조금은 미안하다

내 배는 빈 동굴처럼 생겼지

모든 운동의 중심을 아랫배에만 두고

움직이고 있는 이 소란스런 시간들

저 푸른 화투 패 사이를 비집고

결국, 이 여름 내내 펼쳐지는 올인하는 울음소리

—「매미」 전문

'매미' 라는 기호를 제목으로 달았으니 이 시는 매미의 생애, 그 생태를 이해하면서 읽으면 되겠다. 한여름에 매미 우는 소리를 들으면 정말 '올인' 하고 있다는 느낌이 든다. "모든 운동의 중심을 아랫배에만" 둔 매미라니! 그 모양 또한 선연하다. 매미가 "자신을 다 걸고 덤벼들어도 / 고작 하루를 살아내는 일"인데도 그 하루를 위해 '올인' 하는 존재가 된 것은 그 삶이 그만큼 '절박한 게임' 이 되었기 때문일 것이다. 게다가 나뭇가지 위의 현재의 생명체로 날아오르기 이전의 시간까지 생각하면 그 생은 정말 얼마나 절박한 것인가! 이런 것들을 이해하다 보면 독자들은 이미 이 '매미' 가 단순한 '시적 대상' 에 그치지 않는다는 사실을 알게 된다. '매미' 는 '시적 대상' 이자 그것에 투영된 '절박성' 으로써 이미 '주체로서의 의미' 를 내재한 기호로 기능한다.

'매미'의 '절박성'은 당연히 '사는 것'과 직결돼 있다. 그런데 그것은 곧 '올인하는 울음소리'라는 기표와 '울음으로 표현하는 것이 전부인 삶'이라는 기의로 제공돼 있음을 놓쳐서는 안 된다. 이 시는 박소원 시를 포함한 많은 현대시가 '사는 것'과 '그 사는 것에 대해 표현하는 것'의 '기표/기의'의 관계항 위에 있음을 보여준 예로 제공할 만하다. 다시 좁히면 이 시는 '매미는 왜 그렇게 우는가'라는 질문에 '절박함을 알리기 위해서'라고 대답하는, 즉 '왜 사는가'의 존재론적 물음이자 '왜 쓰는가'의 인문학적 물음에 대해 '절박한 자신의 삶의 모습을 드러냄'이라는 자기 성찰적 대답으로 화답하는 과정으로 이해된다.

3. 카오스에서 코스모스로 가는 노정

현대시는 '표현한 것'과 '그것이 뜻하는 바'의 차이를 심각하게 드러냄으로써 미학적 가치를 획득하는바, 박소원의 시도 스스로 던진 '왜 쓰는가'의 질문에 즉각적인 답으로 호응하지는 않는다. '나의 절박한 삶'에 내재하고 있는 삶의 양상도 단순한 형상화 과정으로 이어지지 않는다.

마음이 먹먹할 때마다
돌들의 무늬를 더듬어보던
내 손 끝에서
들숨일까 날숨일까
파르르 어떤 숨소리가 떨려옵니다
무늬에 따라서 일주일에 한 번
혹은 한 달에 한 번

꽃에 물을 주듯이
내 책장 위에 놓인 돌에게도
물을 주어야겠다는 생각이
그때 문득 들었습니다
처음에는 엉뚱한 생각을 한다고
스스로 도리질을 치곤 했지만
일주일에 한 번 혹은 한 달에 한 번
돌에게 물을 주기 시작하면서
돌이 피우는 꽃을
나는 황홀히 보곤 합니다
먹빛의 몸이 더 먹빛이 되어
베란다 한 귀퉁이에서
이윽고 숨 터지는 저 꽃들
오늘 다시 환하게 만개합니다

당신 안에 살고 있는 돌 한 그루가
기어이 만개하는, 그날이 봄날입니다

—「단단한 꽃」 전문

이 시는 표현한 그대로, '마음의 먹먹함'을 겪는 '나'가 '마음아 너 왜 먹먹해?'라고 자문하고, 그러다가 '그 마음 대신에 눈앞에 보이는 돌'에 물을 주게 되어, 그로부터 '봄꽃의 만개를 획득하는' 과정을 보여준다. 보다 내적인 흐름으로는, 자아('나')를 어떤 대상('돌에서 피는 꽃')을 통해 형상화하면서 하나의 결론('꽃이 만개한 봄날')을 얻은 것으로 이해할 수 있다. 이는 서정시가 지향하는 '자아의 대상화를 통한 정체성 회복' 이라는 가치와 맞닿는다. 그 점에서 이 시에서 '먹먹한 마음의 상태' 에서부터 '꽃이 만개한 봄의 심성' 을 회복하는 일은 곧 '카오스적 상태' 에서 '코스모스적 상태' 를 회복하려는 일련의 과정으로 이해할 수 있다. 이때 '마음아 너 왜 먹먹해?' 라는 자문은 '카오스적 상태' 에 있는 자아에 대한 성찰을 의미하고, 그것은 곧 '왜 쓰는가' 라는 질문과 동질의 것으로 기능한다. 나아가 '코스모스적 상태의 회복' 이라는 가치는 곧 그 질문에 대한 대답이 된다. 박소원의 시는 그러니까 '카오스적 혼란에 빠진 자아' 에 대해 '왜 쓰는가' 로 질문하고 그 답을 얻는 과정에서 '대상화를 통한 형상화' 로써 그 혼란을 정화(淨化)해 결국은 '코스모스적 상태' 에 도달해 가는 노정에 있다.

박소원은 이렇듯 '왜 쓰는가' 자문하고 그 대답으로 '정체성 회복' 을 내세운다. 하지만 이미 앞에서 「매미」를 설명하면서 말했듯이, 카오스 상태의 마음이 '내 마음이 왜 이리 먹먹해?' 하고 질문한다 해서 마냥 코스모스 상태로 진입할 수 있는 것만은 아니다. 설사 그렇게 된다 해도 대체로 시가 보여주는 것은 "울음 하나로 가장 먼 곳까지 나아갔다가 / 가장 가까운 곳으로 돌아오는 나는 누구의 나입니까"(「고사목 4」)로 소리치지만 "새들은 서녘의 말을 물고 / 떠난 자리로 다시 돌아온다"(「나는 다시」)로 되돌아오는 수순에 그친다. 이럴 때 그 시는 '카오스적 상태' 에서 '코스모스적 상태' 를 회복했다는 사실 자체보다 그러한 과정을 전면에 내세우는 양상을 보이게 된다. 즉 그 시는 '왜 쓰는가' 에 대한 질문에 답을 구한 것 이상으로 그 과정을 중시한다는 것이다.

4. 떠도는 기호들의 향연

시인은 시를 쓰며, 그 내면에 '쓴다'는 데 대한 자의식이 크게 자리한다. 그 중에서 어떤 시인은 그 자의식 자체를 크게 문제 삼는다. 박소원이 바로 그렇다고 이미 말했다. 박소원은 쓴다, 그리고 그로부터 '왜 쓰는가'로 자문하는 자아로써 시를 구축해 간다. 박소원의 시는 '쓰는 자의식'으로 가득 차 있다. 쓰는 도구(잉크, 방명록 등), 쓰는 장소(여러 여행지), 쓰는 장르(편지, 일기 등) 등의 변주가 잦은 것도 박소원 시에 '쓰는 자의식'이 점유하는 정도를 짐작케 한다.

> 물이면서도 흐르지 못하는 죄목에 갇혔다
> 강줄기를 따라가거나 폭포수로 내려서 치거나
> 북극의 빙하로 얼어붙는 제 족속들과는
> 소식을 끊고 형벌처럼
> 한 가지 색으로만 짙어가는 시간 속에서
> 저 혼자 고였다 흘렀다 솟구쳤다
> 그 중 순한 속성 하나 붙잡고
> 기록하는 힘, 단 한 가지 색으로
> 융통성 없는 나는 바닥까지 내려가는 중이다
> 하지의 햇빛 한 올이나
> 그믐날 달빛 한 조각도 바람 반 토막도
> 뚜껑 안을 기웃거리다가 한 번 발목을 빠트리면
> 블랙홀처럼 천형 같은
> 암흑의 내면을 빠져나가지 못한다

밖에서 단색들을 움켜쥐고 너무 고독한 걸까
한 방울, 반말처럼 튕겨나가는 불손한 태도들을
그러니 가끔씩 용서해 주시라
계곡이나 강가에 줄지어 선 자작나무 사이를
흘러다니던 자유가
그들의 검은 내벽을 간혹 치는 모양이다
하늘의 일과 강줄기의 일에 더욱 몰두하는 요즘
다만 나는 나의 색을 내어주었을 뿐,
꼼꼼히 기록하는 일은 이제 그들의 뜻이 되었다

—「검은 잉크」에서

이 시에서 '나'는 병 속에 든 '검은 잉크'다. 폭포나 강물처럼 흐르지 못하며, 어떤 빛도 들어오는 순간 암흑에 갇히는 그런 액체 상태다. 하는 일이라곤 '단 한 가지 색'으로 기록하는 것뿐이다. 그런데 그 일, 기록을 실제 하는 것은 '검은 잉크' 자신이 아니라 그것을 펜에 찍어서 쓰는 인간이다. '검은 잉크'는 그것을 사용하는 인간에게 색을 내어주고 그 인간의 '쓰는' 매개로 자리해 있을 수밖에 없다. '단 한 가지 색으로 기록하는 일'밖에 없던 '검은 잉크'로서의 '나'(화자)는 실은 그것을 매개로 새롭게 '꼼꼼히 기록하는 일'을 하는 주체(자아)를 대신하는 기호다. 그런데 이 시는 화자는 뚜렷하되 자아는 제 모습을 유보하고 있다. 주체는 흐릿하고 매개물은 뚜렷하다. 시는 어쩌면 뚜렷한 매개물로 흐릿한 주체를 맴돌게 하는 것인지도 모른다. 과연 이 '검은 잉크'는 그 주인이 된 '그들의 뜻'으로 제대로 쓰일 것인가. 과연 '그들의 뜻'이 있기라도 한 것인가. 그런 건 알 수 없다. '잉크'는 뚜렷하고 그 '주인'은 알 수 없다.

박소원의 시에서 주체는 자주 "등을 떠밀면서 서로를 박박 지워내는 백지의 계절(「백지의 계절에」)" 속을 떠돈다. "말하지 않으면 죽을 것 같은 말들"은 터져나오지 않고 대신 '마른기침'만 터지고 있다(「루마니아의 여름」). 주체를 찾는 매개물만 뚜렷한 모양새로 자꾸 늘어나고, 이 늘어나는 것들이 흐릿하게 떠 있는 주체 주위를 떠돌며 서로 자리를 밀어내면서 때로 주체를 대신하기까지 한다. 주체는 뒤로 물러나 있고 그 대신 대상이 뚜렷한 형상으로 다가오는 세계. 박소원의 시는 주체가 물러나고 대상이 앞서 나오면서 그 대상의 기호들이 펼치는 향연으로 빛난다.

5. 가족사-여행지

박소원 시를 표면에서 장식하는 기호는 거칠게 줄이면 두 가지 성격으로 요약된다. 하나는 자아의 시간 층을 축조해 온 '가족사'이고, 다른 하나는 자아에 현실적 구체성을 불어넣어 주는 '여행'이다.

> 아버지도 어머니도 죽어 나간 시골 집, 우리는 금기를 깨고 같은 자세로 누워 몇 눈금씩 키를 줄인다
>
> 마른 입술로 빽빽이 필사하는 폐가한 가문의 내력을 따라 그믐달은 궁금한 방향으로 몸을 옮기고, 아버지의 그, 여자는 딱딱한 등 뒤에서 쉴 새 없이 지난날을 반성한다
>
> 기억과 기억 사이로 수박 씨앗을 뱉어내듯 끊임없이 쏟아지는 말, 말의 호미질로 새삼 발굴되는 수장된 상처. 그녀와 나 사이에 눈에 보이지 않는 강

하나 흐르기 시작한다

담 밖 사람들에게는 말할 수 없던 시간을 슬쩍 건너 뛸 때마다 우리는 서로의 속으로 첨벙 물길을 트고 있다

첨벙첨벙 제 속으로 떨어지는 물소리에 취해서 쪽잠에 침몰하는 새벽녘, 다음 생엔 평생 너를 봉양하는 효성 깊은 딸로 내가 태어나마

약속인 듯 다짐인 듯 혼잣말을 되뇌이며 엄지손가락이 없는 손이 문득 내 손을 붙잡는다

—「작은어머니」 전문

부모가 타계한 집안에 남은 '아버지의 그, 여자', 즉 '작은어머니'와 한 자리에 누워 대화하는 장면이 펼쳐진다. '나'의 가족은 가부장제에 깊은 뿌리를 둔 대가족이다. 조부의 큰아들인 아버지(「어떤 추억」)는 가부장시대의 장자답게 '작은어머니'를 두었다. 아버지가 '작은어머니'와 차린 살림집에 나가 사는 동안 어머니는 "마른 솔가지를 태워"(「온몸이 귀가 되어」) 저녁밥을 지으며 살고 있다. 그 부모 밑에는 '나'를 포함해 5남 6녀의 자식들이 있으며 그중 한 오빠는 평생 장애를 안고 살았다(「즐거운 장례」). '작은어머니'는 이 가족에 스며든 가부장제의 모순과 대가족 집안의 한을 상징하는 실체다. 아버지가 본가를 두고 그 집에 가서 살았다 해서 '작은어머니'의 생이 편안했을 리 없다. '엄지손가락이 없는 손'은 그 상징물이다. 흥미로운 것은 부모 타계 이후 '나'의 남매들과 '작은어머니'가 한 가족으로 묶여 있었다는 점이다(「즐거운 장례」). '나'와 '작은

어머니'의 '손 붙잡는 대화'는 그 오랜 가족사의 문제를 탐색하게 하는 문이다. 박소원의 많은 시는 그런 문을 통해 자신의 전 생애에 관련한 가족사를 탐색한다. 그것은 '왜 쓰는가'에 대한 답을 찾는 과정으로 펼쳐진다.

나의 희망으로 나는 여기까지 왔다
지극한 슬픔들을 이렇게 묻는다
소란에서 소란으로 소음에서 소음으로
고요에서 고요로 적막에서 적막으로

너와 내가 마주 섰을 때
서서히 일어서는 벽
너와 나 사이 동서로 길게 뻗은 회색 벽 속에는
상처 많은 짐승 한 마리 살고 있다

벽의 균열 속으로 꾸역꾸역
지금껏 걸었던 내 길들을 풀어놓으면
날카로운 늑대의 울음들
수직으로 자라나고
내벽을 후비며 차곡차곡 어둠이 된다

벽은 욱신거리는 울음의 탄력으로
저렇듯 높고 단단해졌다
남프랑스의 새들, 내 파르스름한 입술과
초췌한 빰 위에서 맴돌고 있을 때

슬그머니 벽에 기대어 있으면
땅이 벽을 들어올린 듯
벽 틈바구니가 열리고 늑대의 울음소리들 밖으로 튀어나온다
데굴데굴 겨울나무 사이로 굴러가는 것이다

누구의 희망으로 나는 이곳까지 왔을까
나의 일기는 변명 없이 끝났다
지금부터의 나의 기록은 일기장 밖의 일기들
소란에서 멀리 소음에서 멀리

—「성 폴 요양소 앞에서」 전문

앞선 세 권의 시집이 증명하고 있듯이 박소원의 많은 시는 '여행지' 를 통해 이루어지고 있다. 그 여행지는 중국과 동남아, 러시아와 유럽 전역을 넘나든다. 예니세이 강, 아무르 강, 바이칼 호수, 알혼 섬, 클리아스 강, 코타키나발루 해변 등의 자연의 공간이며 프라하 광장, 북경공항, 칸의 거리, 더블린의 어느 학회 건물 앞 등 도시 공간, 성 폴 요양소, 발자크 박물관, 오베르 교회, 고흐의 무덤 등 유명 유적지 등이 '실제 현장의 시적 자아' 를 유지하게 한다. 장소의 유래도 필요에 따라 거침없이 제공한다. '성 폴 요양소' 는 프랑스의 '생 레미 프로방스에 있는 생 폴 드 모졸 수용소 요양소' 다. '아를에서 25km 떨어진 곳' 으로, 저 유명한 고흐가 스스로 그곳에 와서 '가장 고통스러운 세월' 을 보내면서 수많은 명화를 남겼다' 한다. 이 시에서 명소를 찾는 희망으로 이곳에 온 '나' 는 고흐가 겪은 '가장 고통스러운 세월' 을 자신의 시간으로 이어놓는다. '나' 의 시간은 그동안 '지나온 삶에 대한 나열' 로 성찰되었다. 그런데 그것은 드러

내고 보여주는 것에 그친다는 점에서 진정한 성찰의 단계로 나아간 것으로 볼 수 없다. 진정한 성찰은 드러낸 것 이면에 존재하는지도 모른다. 진정 필요한 것은 기록한 일기가 아니라 그 기록 사이사이에 기록하지 않은 어떤 것, 즉 "일기장 밖의 일기들"이어야 했던 것이다.

일기는 일상이 지나는 때의 기록이다. 시간이 경과할수록 그것은 추억을 되새김질하는 도구이자 지난 사실을 증언하는 증거물이 되기도 한다. 그런데 매일매일 일기를 쓰는데도 쓰지 못한 것이 남아 있었다면? 그때의 일기는 '추억의 되새김질을 위한 도구'로도 '사실의 증거 자료'로도 기능하기 어렵다. 박소원의 시에서 그것은 '자신의 희망을 제대로 담지도 못 했으며' '자신의 삶을 변명해 주지도 못한' 일기로 표현된다. 그런 깨달음을 준 곳이 여행지다.

> 무덤이 없는 곳에서
> 새들은 죽음을 맞이하고
> 먼 곳에서 나는
> 먼 곳에 있는 너를 생각하고 있었다
>
> —「아무르 강가에서」에서

> 참 멀고도 높은 오베르의 교회
> 먼지 희뿌연 방명록에는
> 어느 기록물법에도
> 저촉되지 않는 내생來生의 선약이 적어 있다
>
> —「오베르의 교회 먼지 희뿌연 방명록에」에서

여행은 휴식이자 일탈을 가능하게 하는 행동이다. 그 과정에서 새로운 것을 만나면서 다시 옛 것을 성찰하는 시간을 갖기도 한다. 박소원 시에서 휴식이자 일탈, 새로운 것에 대한 동경과 선망의 행로이던 여행은 회수와 지역을 키워가면서 풍성해지는 외적 대상만큼이나 깊은 내면의 공간을 키우고 있다. "먼 곳에서 나는 / 먼 곳에 있는 너를" 더욱 깊이 생각하게 된 것이다. 그럴수록 그동안의 일기에 없던 진짜 '나'의 얘기가 진정한 일기로 기록되기에 이른다. 그동안의 일기장에 없던 일기, "일기장 밖의 일기"는 "어떤 기록물법에도 저촉"될 리 없는 진정한 기록으로 이어질 것이며 그것은 앞으로의 시간마다 기록되는 '내생(來生)의 선약'으로 자리 잡는다.

6. 거칠고 지친, 새 목소리들

박소원 시에서 '여행지'는 공간적 의미, '가족사'는 시간적 의미로 내재하는데 흥미롭게도 '여행지'의 낯설고 먼 공간적 기운은 '가족사'의 깊은 시간의 층을 헤집는 계기가 된다. 적지 않은 시에서 편지나 일기 등 여행지에서의 '쓰는 행위'가 '가족사의 헤집음'으로 연계되는 걸 확인할 수 있다.

> 내 입에서는 언제부터인가
> 세 사람의 목소리가
> 튀어나온다
>
> 뇌졸중으로 돌아가신 어머니와 태어나서 삼 개월을 살았다는 언니와

마혼에 목매달아 죽은 내 친구, 내 목소리 속 또 다른 목소리들 섞여 나온다

새 발자국 위에
토끼 발자국
토끼 발자국 위에
노루 발자국
노루 발자국 위에
코끼리 발자국처럼
작은 목소리 위에
큰 목소리들이
먼지처럼 덧쌓여간다

비 내리는 창가에 앉아 휘파람을 불거나
주방에서 오리 훈제구이를 굽고 있거나
나에게는 당신의 질병이 유전되고 있다

목소리들, 저승을 이승처럼 이승을 저승처럼 쉴 새 없이 비벼댄다 두고 간 남은 생이 얼마나 그리웠으면 여행지의 마지막 밤까지 따라붙는 거니? 룸메이트는 밤중에 고양이 울음소리가 기분 나쁘다며 창문을 건다 걸쇠를 채운다

이국의 밤은 생수로
칼칼한 목구멍을 헹구고

창밖은 건기의 계절이

슬쩍 우기로 바뀌었다

아, 아

참혹한 전쟁에 패한 병사처럼

거칠고 지친 목소리 아, 아

—「아, 아」 전문

이 시에서 '나'의 현재적 시공은 '이국의 밤'에 자리해 있다. 낯설고 먼 여행지 공간인 만큼 '나'의 '지난 시간 헤집기' 또한 아득하고 골 깊은 층에까지 가닿는다. 그 층에서 "뇌졸중으로 돌아가신 어머니", "태어나서 삼 개월을 살았다는 언니", "마흔에 목매달아 죽은 친구" 등 세 사람이 '내 입의 목소리'로 튀어나온다. 그것들은 "저승을 이승처럼 이승을 저승처럼 쉴 새 없이 비벼댄다." 몸은 '룸메이트와 함께 한 침실'에 와 있는데 '나'의 내면은 '이승과 저승을 넘나드는 가족의 시간'을 헤집고 있는 것이다. '세 사람 목소리'라 했지만 그것에 그치지 않고, 그 넘나듦의 층에 작은 것, 큰 것, 새 토끼 노루 코끼리로 기표되는 무수한 것들이 함께 묻어나온다. '내 목소리'이자 '세 사람 목소리'이자 '시간의 층 곳곳에 스민 목소리'를 아우른다.

박소원 시는 집에서 멀어지는 여행과 그것에서 깊어지는 시간 탐색으로 '나-자아-화자'가 발화하는 기표를 끊임없이 생산해 낸다. 그로써 자문-자답으로 이어지는 자기성찰의 시적 세계를 일구어 왔다. 자기성찰은 대체로 자기치유의 과정이 되는 법이고 박소원 시에서도 그것은 '카오스적 혼돈'에서 '코스모스적 세계'를 회복하는 정화 과정을 보여왔다. 그러나 그 과정에서 박소원 시는 미처 기록하지 못한 더 많은 시간 층을 발견하고 여전한 탐색의 과정에 서 있다. 이미 지나온 줄 알았지만 다시 지나가야 생이 그 앞에 아직 두텁게 놓여 있는 셈이다. 그렇다면 시인은 '거칠고 지친 목소리' 이지만 그걸 '새 목소리' 로 내야 할 터. 그것이 시인의 숙명 아닐까. '지난 시간' 이지만 외면할 수 없는 시간이라면 그것은 앞으로 살아가야 하는 내생(來生)과 다름없는 것, 박소원의 시는 이제 그 내생의 기록을 향할 수밖에 없다.

A review

For the Record of Next Life

— the poems by Park So Won

Park Duk Kyu(Poet, Literary Critic)

I. Asking "Why write?"

"Why write?" one asks. It is the question posed to those who write and those who are aspiring to write. Both the writers and the would-be writers ask it. The answers have been numerous and various, but even those who did not answer as well as those who did, also ask. They ask again and again. "Why do I write?" Park So Won asks herself. No, I want to ask Park So Won. "Why do you write?"

Since her debut in the literary world in 2004, Park So Won has published three poetry collections: *Is There a Memory as Warm as Sorrow?*(2010), *Postcards Written in Xihu Park*(2013), and *A Joyful Funeral*(2021). There are also quite a lot of poems that didn't make it into these collections. And yet she continues to write. Being a poet means being one who writes, and though three poetry collections might generally be the sum a poet achieves in her lifetime, I still feel compelled to ask Park So Won. "Why do you write?" Park So Won is also asking herself. "Why do I write?" And she answers herself.

The resolution to forget has again become a false vow.
A familiar name, thrown out of the window of the train to Siberia,
When I arrive at the island, it is floating with the stars in the bright night.

On the vivid blue back of the postcard I write that it's a nearby place,
And beneath it, add it's a distant place.

I write that I eat a fish called omul* at every meal,
Adding that it seems to be a species between saury and mackerel.

I write that I may arrive earlier than the postcard,
And then lie stretched out on a pool chair, closing my eyes.

People sitting on the grass, looking for a four-leaf clover,
walking down to the blue lake,
and going up to the observatory

whose directions of paths are different, as are the dwellings of souls.

In the evening when the sun never sets,
wearing black sunglasses,
smiling only with mouth,
eating,
drinking tea,
and drinking vodka;
it's a dreamlike reality
in this unfamiliar land of fairy tales.

The time when even if I fall alseep, words never become fewer.
I cannot keep silent during this beautiful moment,
so I write that I pick yellow flowers and place them between the pages of the map of Lake Baikal.

With a hand that hurts and aches, I write and write again.
Without tears, I still have news to say to you.

— "Postcard Written from Olkhon Island"

The theme of 'writing' in Park So Won's poetry often appears in contexts where 'I' directly record something, such as in letters or diaries. In the passage above, 'I' am writing a postcard. Naturally, it is because there is 'news to tell' to 'you,' the recipient. However, 'writing a postcard' in this context does not simply refer to the actual act of writing but to this poem itself and to the very act of writing this poem, representing 'writing a postcard'. The 'news to tell' cannot be the fact that 'I,' who is far away, sends a letter written with "a hand that hurts and aches." Rather, the 'news to tell' in the letter (postcard) refers to what is communicated, the 'content of utterance' within the relationship between 'I-the speaker' and 'you-the poetic listener' of the poem, which is the signifier/signified of that. As poetry traditionally creates value through the process of understanding the signified through the signifier, many of Park So Won's poems are imbued with the process of highlighting the 'signified as the news to tell,' which is the purpose of the act of 'writing,' by emphasizing the 'signifier.' In short, this poem aims not to reveal 'the news written painfully' but to expose 'the very act of writing painfully itself.' References like "the train to Siberia", "blue lake", "Olkhon Island', "observatory" mentioned in the poem serve as the spatial backdrop and the actual places from which 'I-the speaker' narrates, enhancing the reality of the 'painful atmosphere.'

II. Ontology - Self-Reflection

The fact that Park So Won's poetry reveals a process of self-questioning 'Why do I write?' and answering that question can be easily seen in other poems, not just in cases like the above where the act of actual writing is used as a signifier.

> Tucked between branches and gaps,
> Opening and closing hearts like sliding doors,
> I spend an entire season.
> Mae-em Mae-em Me-e-em,*
> At any time, until my vocal cords burst from strain,
> Looking into the cracks in my body
> Where strange sounds escape,
> Today, too, word by word
> I'm learning the art of living through crying.
> The strange sounds of crying,
> Quietly detecting the sensor of crying
> Which operates like the instinct of life
> To move linking with the movement of the body,
> And hiding under the bark of the trees during the day,
> And pops out at night,
> No one realizes this is a desperate game
> Played by risking all of me.
> Even throwing himself all in,
> It is just to live out a day,
> Tut tut tut, I feel a bit sorry for myself for a gamble.
> My belly looks like an empty cave.

These noisy times moving,

When focusing the center of all movements

On the lower abdomen;

Wedging through the blue cards of hwatoo**

Finally, the all-in cries unfolding throughout this summer.

— "Cicada"

Since the poem is titled "Cicada", it should be read in the context of the cicada's life and its natural behavior. Hearing the cicada's cry in the height of summer gives a real sense of it being 'all in.' Imagine a cicada "focusing the center of all movements / On the lower abdomen"! Its form is also vivid. Although the cicada "Even throwing itself all in / It is just to live out a day", it becomes a being that goes 'all in' for that day because its life has become such a 'desperate game.' Furthermore, if you consider the time before it emerged as a living creature on the branch, how desperate must its life be! Understanding these elements, readers realize that this 'Cicada' is not merely a 'poetic object.' It functions as a sign that inherently carries 'meaning as a subject,' representing 'desperation' projected onto it.

The 'desperation' of the 'Cicada' is naturally connected to 'living.' However, we should remember that it serves as a signifier of 'all-in crying' and the signified of 'a life where expressing through crying is everything.' This poem serves as an example that many modern poems, including those by Park So Won, exist on the relationship between the 'signifier/signified' of 'living' and 'expressing that living.' Narrowing it down, this poem answers the question, 'Why does the cicada cry so?' with 'to notify desperation,' thus responding both to the ontological question of 'Why live?' and to the humanistic question of 'Why write?' with a self-reflective answer that 'reveals the desperate aspects of its own life.'

III. On the Way from Chaos to Cosmos

As modern poetry acquires aesthetic value by seriously revealing the difference between 'what is expressed' and 'what it means', Park So Won's poetry does not immediately respond to the self-posed question 'Why write?' The aspects of 'my desperate life' inherent within do not lead to a simple process of forming an image.

> Whenever my heart feels down and gloomy,
> From my fingertips,
> Tracing the patterns of the stones,
> A trembling breath, whether an inhalation or exhalation,
> Comes fluttering.
> Depending on the pattern, once a week,

Or once a month,

Like watering flowers,

Suddenly I thought

I should water the stones on my bookshelf.

At first, I shook my head

For the absurd thought,

But since I started watering the stones

Once a week or once a month,

I have ecstatically observed the flowers

They are blooming.

Those flowers, whose dark bodies become even darker,

Bursting out of breath at last

In the corner of the veranda,

Are blooming full bright again today.

The day when a stone living inside you

Finally blossoms, that day is spring.

— "Solid Flower"

This poem, as expressed, shows the 'I' experiencing "down and gloomy" feelings, asking 'Heart, why are you so down and gloomy?' and then, instead of dwelling on this feeling, ends up watering a stone seen before them, leading to spring flowers "blooming fully and brightly." As to the internal flow of this poem, this can be understood as the self ('I') shaping an identity through an object ("the flowers they, the stones, are blooming") and reaching a conclusion ('a spring day with blooming flowers'). This accords with the lyrical poetry's aim of 'restoring identity through the objectification of the self.' From this point, the journey from a "down and gloomy" state to 'a spring spirit of full bloom' can be seen as a series of process from a 'chaotic state' to a 'cosmic state.' Here, the self-query "Heart, why do you feel down and gloomy?" signifies a reflection on the self in a chaotic state, akin to the question 'Why write?' The value of 'recovering a cosmic state' then becomes the answer to the question. Park So Won's poetry, therefore, questions the 'self in chaotic turmoil' with 'Why write?' and in the process of finding the answer, purifies the turmoil through 'forming through objectification,' eventually trying to reach a 'cosmic state.'

Park So Won, thus, questions herself with 'Why write?' and offers 'restoring identity' as the answer. However, as previously mentioned with "cicada", just because the heart in a chaotic state asks, "Why does my heart feel so down and gloomy?" does not mean it can easily come into a cosmic state. Even if it does, what the poetry typically shows is that the narrator shouts with a cry as in "Who am I, who reaches the farthest place with a single cry"(from "Dead Tree - 4") and returning to the starting point as in "Birds carry the words of the west / Coming back to wherh they left" (from "I, Once

Again"). At such times, the poem brings more the process to the forefront than merely stating the recovery from a 'chaotic state' to a 'cosmic state.' That is, the poem values the process higher than simply answering the question 'Why write?'

Ⅳ. A Feast of Wandering Signs

The poet, while writing, harbors a strong self-consciousness about the act of 'writing.' Some poets particularly problematize this self-consciousness itself. As already stated, Park So Won is one of such poets. Park So Won writes, and from that, constructs her poetry as a self that self-questions 'Why write?' Her poems are filled with 'the self-consciousness of writing', which is evident from the frequent variations in writing tools(ink, guest books), places of writing(various travel destinations), and genres(letters, diaries). It indicates the extent to which this 'the self-consciousness of writing' occupies her poetry.

I am water, yet trapped in the crime of being unable to flow,
Cut off from my kin, who follow river currents, crash down waterfalls,
Or freeze into Arctic glaciers,
Like a punishment,
Alone, I pooled, flowed, and soared up.

In a time when it deepened into a single hue.
Clutching at one mild characteristic
With the power to record, with just one color,
Inflexible, I am sinking to the bottom.
Neither a ray of sunlight at the summer solstice
Nor a silver moonlight on the last day, not even a breath of wind can escape
If it slips its ankle while peeking beneath the lid,
It can't escape the darkness inside,
Like divine punishment akin to a black hole.

Am I too lonely outside, clutching monochromes tightly?
So, occasionally forgive me —
A drop of impertinent attitude that bounces off like informal speech.
The freedom that once flowed between rows of birch trees
By the valley or riverside
Seems to strike sometimes their black inner walls.
These days, absorbed much in the things of the sky and the rivers.
I merely gave away my color,
Now it became their will to keep meticulous records.

— from "Black Ink"

In this poem, 'I' am the 'black ink' in a bottle, unable to

flow like a waterfall or river, and am a liquid which traps any light that comes it in darkness. All I do is record in "just one color." However, it is not the "black ink" itself but the human being who dips it in a pen and writes that does the actual act of recording. "Black ink" merely provides color for the human being's use, serving as a medium for her 'writing.' The 'I' (the speaker) as 'black ink,' with no ability but to record in 'just one color,' actually represents the agent (self) who "keeps meticulous records" through this medium. Yet in this poem, the speaker is distinct while the self remains reserved. The agent is blurred, and the medium is clear. Perhaps the poem circles around a blurred agent with a distinct medium. Will this "black ink" be used properly according to 'its(master's) intention'? Whether 'the master's intention' even exists is unknown. 'Ink' is clear, but its 'owners' are unknowable.

In Park So Won's poetry, subjects often drift through a "season of blank paper, erasing each other as they push against each other's backs."(from 'Season of Blank Paper')." The words "that I was eager to burst out" do not burst forth, but instead, only "a dry cough broke out"(from "The Summer in Romania"). The number of distinct mediums searching for a subject keeps increasing, and these expanding entities sometimes substitute for the blurry subject as they float around and jostle for position. In this world, the subject recedes and, in its place, the object approaches in a distinct form. Park So Won's poetry shines as a feast laid out by the signs of these foregrounded objects, while the subject recedes.

V. Family History – Travel

The symbols that decorate the surface of Park So Won's poetry can roughly be summarized into two categories. One is 'family history,' which constructs the layers of the self's time, and the other is 'travel,' which breathes realistic concreteness into the self.

> In the countryside house, where both father and mother died, we break the taboo and lower ourselves by a few scales lying in the same posture;
>
> Following the genealogy of our ruined family, we diligently copy with dry lips. Meanwhile the waning moon moves in a curious direction. Behind my father's stiff back, the woman, his lady, reflects incessantly on the past;
>
> Words poured out incessantly like watermelon seeds spat out between memories, and newly unearthed water-buried wounds by the hoe of words. An invisible river starts to flow between her and me;

Whenever skipping over the times, we couldn't speak to those outside the walls, we splash into each other's hearts;

Intoxicated by the sound of water splashing into itself

And sinking into a dawn nap, I promise that in the next life I will be born as a dutiful daughter, caring for you throughout my life;

Repeating this to herself, as if making a promise or a resolution, her hand without a thumb suddenly grips mine.

— "Little Mother"

In the house left after the parents' demise, there unfolds a scene where 'I' lies in bed conversing with 'my father's woman,' referred to as 'little mother.' 'I' come from a large family deeply rooted in patriarchy. My father, the eldest son of my grandfather (from "A Certain Memory"), fittingly for the convention of his era, had a 'little mother.' While my father lived in a separate household with the 'little mother,' my mother was at home "burning dry pine branches" (from "Becoming All Ears") to cook dinner. Under these parents, there were seven children, two boys and five girls, including 'me,' and one of my brothers lived with a lifelong disability(from "A Joyful Funeral"). The "little mother" is a reality that symbolizes the contradictions of patriarchy ingrained in our large family. It's unlikely that her life was comfortable, even though my father lived with her in her house. The metaphor of a 'hand without a thumb' symbolizes her hard situation. What is interesting is that after the parents passed away, 'my' siblings and the 'little mother' were bound together as one family(from "A Joyful Funeral"). The 'hand-holding conversation' between 'me' and the 'little mother' opens a door to exploring the longstanding issues of her family history. Many of Park So Won's poems explore through such gates her entire life's family history, which is revealed as a process to find the answer to 'Why write?'

With my hope, I have come here.
I bury such extreme sorrows
from turmoil to turmoil, from noise to noise,
from silence to silence, from desolation to desolation.

When you and I stood face to face,
a wall slowly rising
between you and me, in this long grey wall stretching east to west,
a beast lives with many wounds.

Into the cracks in the wall, laboriously,
if I let go of the paths I've walked till now,

the sharp cries of wolves
rise vertically,
and scratching the inner walls, gradually become darkness.

The wall has grown high and solid,
with the elasticity of throbbing cries.
When the birds of Southern France hover
over my pale lips and gaunt cheeks.

If I lean slowly against the wall,
as if the earth has lifted the wall,
a gap in the wall opens and the cries of wolves leap out of it,
rolling between the winter trees.

With whose hope did I come this far?
My diary ended without excuses.
My records from now on are diaries outside the diary,
far from turmoil, far from noise.

— "In Front of the Saint Paul Asylum"

As evidenced by the previous three volumes of poetry, many of Park's poems are published through 'travel destinations'. The destination crosses China and Southeast Asia, Russia and Europe. Natural spaces such as the Yenisei River, Amur River, Lake Baikal, Olkhon Island, Klias River, Kota Kinabalu

Beach, etc., are maintained as "the poetic self of the real world" by city spaces such as Prague Plaza, Peking Airport, Cannes Street, in front of a conference building in Dublin, St. Paul's Sanatorium, the Balzac Museum, the Aubert Church, and Gogh's Tomb. The origin of the place is also provided without hesitation as needed. The St. Paul's Asylum is a Sanctuary for the St. Paul de Mozzol concentration camp in St. Remy Provence in France. "25 km away from Arles", it is the place where that famous Gogh came by himself and spent the 'most painful years' leaving numerous famous paintings. Having come here with the hope of finding a famous place in the city, 'I' continue the 'most painful years' that Gogh has experienced into her own time. 'My time' has been reflected on 'a list of the lives that have passed.' However, it cannot be seen as a step forward for true reflection in that it is limited to revealing and showing. True reflection may exist behind what was revealed. What was really needed was not a written diary, but something not recorded in between, namely, "diaries outside the diary."

A diary is a record of the passage of daily life. As time passes, it becomes both a tool to reflect on memories and evidence to testify of past facts. But what if there was something you couldn't write even though you kept a diary every day? The diary at that time is difficult to function as a "tool for reflecting on memories" or "evidence of facts." In Park

So Won's poem, it is expressed as a diary that "failed to properly contain one's hopes" and "failed to excuse one's life." It is the travel destination that gives such enlightenment.

> In a place where there are no graves,
> Birds face death,
> And from afar, I was
> Thinking of you, who were also far away.
> — from "By the Amur River"

> The church of Auvers, so distant and lofty,
> in its dusty, faint guestbook,
> is soaked with a prior commitment from my forthcoming life,
> violating no archival law.
> — from "In the Dusty, Faint Guestbook of the Church in Auvers"

Travel is an act that allows both relaxation and deviation. In the process, it provides a time to encounter new things while reflecting on the old. In the poems of Park So Won, travel which is a path of yearning and admiration for rest, deviation, and new things, enhances both the richness of external objects and the depth of internal spaces as it expands revisits and adds the regions. "From afar, I was / Thinking of you, who were also far away" more than ever. As this experience occurs repeatedly, the stories of the real 'me,' previously absent from past diaries, become recorded as true diaries. These diarys which can not be written in the past diary, "diaries outside the diary," "violating no archival law", will continue as true records and serve as a "a prior commitment from my forthcoming life" in every moment ahead.

Ⅵ. Rough and Weary, New Voices

In Park So Won's poems, 'travel destinations' possess a spatial significance, while 'family history' is emboded as a temporal meaning. Interestingly, the unfamiliar and distant atmosphere of 'travel destinations' serves as occurences that dig out the deep layers of 'family history.' It's evident in numerous poems how writing activities like letters or diaries at travel destinations are linked to the digging out of 'family history.'

From my mouth, for some time now,
voices of three people
spring forth.

My mother, who passed away from a stroke, my sister, who lived for only three months after birth,

and my friend who hung himself at forty, their voices mix with mine and emerge from within.

Like elephant footprints
on top of deer footprints
on top of rabbit footprints
on fresh snow,
large voices
pile up on the small ones
like layers of dust.

I, Sitting by the window on a rainy day whistling,
or cooking duck confit in the kitchen,
your diseases are being passed down to me.

Voices, tirelessly blending the hereafter with the here and now, the here and now with the hereafter, how much must they have missed the life they left behind to cling to me until the last night of a journey? My roommate closes the window in the middle of the night, finding the sound of a cat's cry unsettling, and locks it.

The night in a foreign land washes my spicy throat with bottled water,
and outside, the dry season
slyly turns into the rainy season.
Ah, ah,

like a soldier defeated in a terrible war,

a rough and tired voice, ah, ah.

— "Ah, Ah"

In this poem, the "I" exists in the present time-space of "a foreign night." As the location is a strange and distant travel destination, the "I"'s "digging out past times" reaches into deep and profound layers. From these layers, three figures emerge as "voices from my mouth": "a mother who passed away from a stroke," "my sister, who lived for only three months after birth," and "my friend who hung himself at forty." These voices "tirelessly blending the hereafter with the here and now, and the here with the hereafter." While the body is in a bedroom with a roommate, the "I"'s inner self is digging out the family's time that crosses the boundaries of the living and the dead. Although referred to as 'three voices,' the interaction doesn't stop there; logs of small and large entities, signified by rabbits, deer, and elephants, also emerge from this transcendental layer. It includes the 'voice of mine', 'the three voices' and the 'voices infused throughout the layers of time.'

Park So Won's poetry produces continuous signifiers that the "I-self-speaker" utters, deepened by travel away from home and the exploration of time. Through self-questioning and answering, she has cultivated her own unique poetic world of self-reflection. Generally, self-reflection leads to a process of self-healing, and in Park So Won's poetry, this shows a purification process from 'chaotic disorder' to a 'cosmological world.' However, in this process, Park So Won's poetry discovers more unrecorded layers of time, and she is still in the midst of ongoing exploration. Believed to have been passed, life still lies thickly ahead she has to overcome once more. Thus, the poet, with 'a voice both rough and weary', should try to utter new voices. That is perhaps the poet's destiny. If the 'past time' cannot be ignored, it is no other than the future life she must live. Park So Won's poetry is now inevitably headed for recording this next life. (the End)

박소원 한영시집

아, 아

Ah, Ah

초판 1쇄 발행 2024년 7월 12일

지은이 박소원
옮긴이 여국현
펴낸이 임현경

펴낸곳 곰곰나루
출판등록 제2019－000052호 (2019년 9월 24일)
주소 서울특별시 양천구 목동서로 221 굿모닝탑 201동 605호(목동)
전화 02－2649－0609
팩스 02－798－1131
전자우편 merdian6304@naver.com
유튜브 채널 곰곰나루

ISBN 979－11－92621－14－2 03810

책값 15,000원